About the Author

Len Driscoll is the pen name for author **Frank Dirscherl**, best known for his many novels in *The Wraith Dread Avenger of the Underworld* series, including the Amazon bestselling *The Wraith* and *Sanderson of Metro,* as well as several short stories. *The Magpie's Shadow* is the third in the *George 'Magpie' Collins mystery* series.

A librarian with over thirty years experience, Frank has also worked at a book wholesaler, a specialist medical practice and as a tutor in the writing and producing of comic books. His interests include reading, traveling, politics, architecture and the environment.

Frank lives in the Illawarra on the south coast of New South Wales, Australia, with his wife and daughter, and is always working on his latest literary endeavors.

Praise for *Sanderson of Metro*
Amazon bestseller

"Once shrouded in mystery, The Wraith's stunning origin is finally revealed. Dirscherl and Nash have written one hell of an adventure novel filled with myth, intrigue, and excitement. Highly recommended reading."
  – A.P. Fuchs, writer, *The Axiom-man Saga, The Way of the Fog, Undead World trilogy*

"Recommended for Wraith and pulp hero fans."
  – Leon Mallett, *Amazon*

"At the end of the day, this novel is a worthy addition to The Wraith's continuing story and a necessary purchase if you're a fan of the character. It's also just a flat out enjoyable reading experience."
  – Marcus Bucklin, *Amazon*

"The story is well written, and the Paul Sanderson character fleshed out fairly well...I highly recommend this well written entry for all comic book fans."
  – Virginia E. Johnson, *Amazon*

Praise for *The Wraith*
Amazon bestseller

"I love the coloring job and specially the 'glowing' eyes on the chest of the character."
- Guillermo del Toro, director, *Blade II, Hellboy I & II*

"I liked the story a lot... It's a very strong debut."
Steve Englehart, writer, *Detective Comics, The Avengers, Green Lantern*

"I have read the novel (I couldn't put it down)... It is amazing to see how her (Leena) character evolves from Part I to Part II. At first she appears as every other 'girlfriend' in an action film, but those twelve months that pass obviously change her as a person and I love the person she becomes: tougher, but still human."
- Amber Moelter, actress, *Catwoman: Copycat*

"I finished *The Wraith* book last night. I must say I enjoyed it quite a bit. The scenes kept playing in my head like a big budget Hollywood film. I mentioned earlier that I enjoy when the hero is put to the test physically and doesn't win the battle unscathed. Boy, (Frank) delivered that in spades!"
- Jeff Welborn, artist, *Nightmare World, The Wraith*

"Genius + sweat + dedication = hard hittin' hero action! Go Aussie!"
- Dan Lennard, writer, *People* magazine

"*The Wraith* is a wonderful throwback to the purple prose of the bloody pulps with a hero clearly descendant from the likes of the Shadow and the Spider. A fast, action-packed thrill-ride with great characters, both noble and villainous. Slam-bang kick off to a super new series. One I'm anxious to follow."

   – Ron Fortier, writer, *The Spider, Brother Bones, Domino Lady*

"I became familiar with Frank Dirscherl's The Wraith from the comic book of the same name. When the first Wraith novel came out I just had to read it. I was not disappointed. The Wraith is a fast-paced thrill-ride. I'm looking forward to the upcoming sequel."

   – Bobby Nash, writer, *Evil Ways, Fantastix, Lance Star*

"*The Wraith* (is) a really fun read. Have been a fan of Kenneth Robeson's Doc Savage and The Avenger books for years... *The Wraith* reminds me of Robeson at his best."

   – G.R. Lawson, Publisher, General Jinjur Comics

"A short, pulp, superhero novel... Clearly more adventures to come with how this is set up."

   – Richard Scott, *Super Reader* website

"*The Wraith* is an enlightening journey into the darkness of superhero fiction, and a worthy entry into both pulpdom and comicdom."

   – Kevin Noel Olson, *Silver Bullet Comics* website

Praise for *Valley of Evil*

"The second Wraith novel is an improvement, I think. Right from the start Dirscherl throws you into the middle of crazy action.... This book is a whole lot of superheroic pulp fun, and the good news is there seems to be more to come...I look forward to some more of the same."

> – Richard Scott, *Super Reader* website

"I think (Dirscherl) really captured a noir element with (his) voice."

> – Joshua Gamon, writer, *Abigail & Rox, Digital Webbing Presents*

"I did quite enjoy the books. Best of all, it wasn't overly sex-filled or gory—I can't stand most modern superhero comics that show such things or have the heroes just swear and swear. So *The Wraith* (and *Valley of Evil*) was just up my alley."

> – Greg Gick, writer, *The Werewolf of Rutherford Grange, Tales of the Shadowmen, Secret Agent X Vol. 2*

"The Dread Avenger is back. After battling the Cobra in his first prose adventure, The Wraith returns to face all new challenges from Metro City's greatest villains, most notably Hong Kong drug kingpin Ma Tzi. As with his first Wraith novel, Frank Dirscherl treats us to a pulp-inspired adventure that keeps readers on the edge of their seat. You have to read this novel in one sitting."

> – Bobby Nash, writer, *Evil Ways, Fantastix, Lance Star*

"In the past five years there has been a tremendous resurgence in pulp fiction centering on the old heroic pulps. Young writers have started taking up the mantle of old masters like Walter Gibson and Lester Dent and begun creating their own avengers in tales of genuine purple prose. Among the best of this new generation of wordsmiths is Australian, Frank Dirscherl and the exploits of his modern pulp paladin, The Wraith. This is grand pulp!"

- Ron Fortier, writer, *The Spider, Brother Bones, Domino Lady*

Praise for *Crossfire*

"Stephen did a fantastic job of bringing Frank Dirscherl's character to life!"
  – Adam DiTroia, composer, *The Wraith: Eyes of Judgment*,
MTV, Fox Sports

"Loved the book!! Can't wait for the next installment…"
  – Larry Mainland, actor, *The Walking Dead, Lawless,
The Three Stooges*

"The action comes swift, and doesn't stop until the final pages. *Crossfire* tells a great story of betrayal and revenge."
  – C.R. Blevins, writer, *A Western Tale*

"This was my first introduction to The Wraith and I was not disappointed. The action comes swift, and doesn't stop until the final pages…. If you love a good action/hero story, you will certainly enjoy reading *Crossfire*."
  – Ally, *Amazon*

"Makes me want more…should be the next series on Netflix…"
  – Bill Lancaster, *Amazon*

"Another excellent entry in The Wraith Adventures series. Thoroughly recommended for Wraith fans and fans of pulp super-heroics."
  – Leon Mallett, *Amazon*

Praise for *Cult of the Damned*

"Only by the first three pages, Frank Dirscherl wonderfully captures a dark and mysterious atmosphere, one that leaves the reader with a cryptic and eerie sensation; one that makes me cold just thinking about it."

> – Rennie Cowan, writer/director, *The Thriller Idol: A Tribute to the Legacy of Michael Jackson, Kade the Conqueror*

"Frank Dirscherl pulls you into the world of The Wraith from the first sentence and refuses to let you go until the last one."

> – Stephen J. Semones, writer/director, *Beyond the Lens, Crossfire, The Wraith: Eyes of Judgment*

"The Wraith is one of my favorite characters and every time Frank Dirscherl puts pen to paper I know I'm in for a real treat."

> – A.P. Fuchs, writer, *The Axiom-man Saga, The Way of the Fog, Undead World trilogy*

Praise for *Cry of the Werewolf*

"Frank Dirscherl delivers beyond measure.... The solid characters, settings and story really propel you page to page and leave you hanging on for more."

> – Stephen J. Semones, writer/director, *Beyond the Lens, Crossfire, The Wraith: Eyes of Judgment*

"Each new installment in *The Wraith Adventures* series is a guaranteed good time filled with high adventure, romance and pulpy fun. Dirscherl is at the top of his form."

> – A.P. Fuchs, writer, *The Axiom-man Saga, The Way of the Fog, Undead World trilogy*

"The writing is well done and well edited, and is filled with that distinct Dirscherl style of pulp that I enjoy so much. The book is a perfect example of what Neo Pulp/Superhero and Horror fiction can be and is a worthy addition to any fan's collection."

> – Marcus Bucklin, *Amazon*

Praise for *Vendetta*

"...in all a great brew that had me hooked for the whole ride. Now bring on the next book, Frank..."

– Leon Mallett, Amazon

"This book starts with a literal bang and doesn't let the foot off of the gas until the very last page. The book is well plotted and moves at a breakneck pace, making it an enjoyable, short read. I loved this book very much as a fan of The Wraith and I believe that anyone who is a fan of the series should consider this required reading."

– Marcus Bucklin, Amazon

Praise for *Zombies Attack!* in *Metahumans vs the Undead*

"This compilation of superheroes vs evil offers top entertainment for superhero lovers! Frank Dirscherl and others are at their best with their contributed stories. I will now pursue other stories written by these authors, such as those involving Mr Dirscherl's The Wraith. This type of reading enjoyment knows no end!"

> –   Ramona Wingart, writer, *Where is Brother Beaver?*,
> *Emily Suzanne Smith!*

BY LEN DRISCOLL

FICTION

the *George 'Magpie' Collins mystery* series

1. *The Broken Chain*
2. *The Black Seam*
3. *The Magpie's Shadow*
4. *The Lost Boy* - COMING SOON

BY FRANK DIRSCHERL

The Wraith Dread Avenger of the Underworld series

1. *The Wraith*
2. *Valley of Evil*
3. *Crossfire* (with Stephen J. Semones)
4. *Cult of the Damned*
5. *Cry of the Werewolf*
6. *Swamp Witch of Satan's Forest* (with Ray MacKay)
7. *Vendetta*
8. *Lady Wraith* (with Adam Oravec)
9. *Kingdom*
10. *City of Fear*
11. *Birds of the Living Dead*
12. *The Acolyte* - COMING SOON

Books of Judgment

1. *Sanderson of Metro* (with Bobby Nash)
2. *Serpent Rising* (with Greg Gick)
3. *Rising Son* (with Adam Oravec) - COMING SOON

SHORT STORY COLLECTIONS

The Wraith Vol. 1
The Wraith Vol. 2 - COMING SOON
Lance Star – Sky Ranger Vol. 1

NON-FICTION

The Hitchers of Oz
Beyond the Lens (edited)

THE MAGPIE'S SHADOW

a George 'Magpie' Collins mystery #3

by

Len Driscoll

GLOWING EYES MEDIA
WOLLONGONG

GLOWING EYES MEDIA
PO Box 31
Wollongong NSW 2520

ISBN 978-0-646-73033-2

THE MAGPIE'S SHADOW

PUBLISHED BY GLOWING EYES MEDIA, November 2025
www.glowingeyesmedia.com
FRONT COVER ART by Chaz Gupta
COVER LAYOUT AND DESIGN AND INTERIOR DESIGN by Frank Dirscherl
EDITED by Claude Aylmer
FIRST EDITION

For more on *The Magpie's Shadow*
visit www.glowingeyesmedia.com

Text set in Garamond-Normal. Printed and bound in the USA

A catalogue record for this book is available from the National Library of Australia

To my family...you are my everything

THE MAGPIE'S
SHADOW

~ Chapter 1 ~

A cold winter rain drummed against the grimy windows of my second-floor office like impatient fingers tapping on a bar top. I sat behind my desk, nursing a cup of black coffee that had gone cold an hour ago, watching the water streak down the glass in irregular patterns that reminded me of the tears on a fence's face when the coppers finally caught up with him. The view from my window on Castlereagh Street wasn't much—just the wet brick wall of the building opposite and a narrow slice of grey Sydney sky that promised more rain before the day was through.

It was Thursday, the fifteenth of July, 1935, and business had been slower than a funeral procession. The sign on my door read 'George Collins, Private Investigator' in faded gold lettering that had seen better days. I used to work outside the law, as a jewel thief of some little renown. In those days, my nickname had been 'Magpie', due to my predilection for all things sparkly. Nowadays, the only one who still called me that was my good friend, Police Chief Tom Majors, the man who helped me see sense and assisted in my acquiring my investigator's licence. These days, my particular knowledge of criminal behaviour came in handy in helping the law-abiding citizens of Sydney solve their problems, though the irony wasn't lost on me that I was now paid to catch the sort of bloke I used to be.

The rain had been falling steadily for three days, turning the streets into rivers and keeping most sensible people indoors. I'd spent the morning reading the day's '*Sydney Morning Herald'* and trying to make sense of the political situation in Europe, where that Austrian madman with the Charlie Chaplin moustache was making increasingly unpleasant noises about his neighbours. Closer to home, the Labor Party was making headway in the state parliament, which suited me fine. I'd always believed that a fair day's work deserved a fair day's pay, and that the bloke in the expensive suit shouldn't get rich off the sweat of the working man's brow.

I was contemplating whether to venture next door to the NSW Masonic Club for a late breakfast when I heard footsteps in the corridor outside my office. They were light, measured steps—a woman's heels clicking against the worn linoleum with the kind of precision that spoke of breeding and money. The footsteps paused outside my door, and I heard the rustle of clothing as someone read the nameplate. A moment later, a soft knock echoed through the room.

"Come in," I called, straightening my tie and pushing the newspaper aside.

The door opened to reveal a woman who belonged in the society pages of the newspaper rather than in the shabby office of a reformed criminal turned private detective. She was somewhere in her forties, I estimated, with dark auburn hair styled in perfect waves and a complexion that spoke of regular visits to expensive beauty salons. Her navy blue dress was cut from expensive fabric and tailored to perfection, and she carried herself with the kind of poise that comes from never having to worry about where her next meal was coming from. Everything about her screamed money, from the pearl earrings that caught the grey light from the window to the crocodile leather handbag she clutched in gloved hands.

But it was her eyes that caught my attention. They were a striking shade of blue, the colour of sapphire, and they held a combination of desperation and determination that I'd seen before in clients who had nowhere else to turn. She stood in the doorway for a moment, taking in the spartanly furnished office with its well-used desk, two excellent though equally well-used chairs, and filing cabinet that had seen better decades.

"Mr Collins?" she asked, her voice carrying the refined accent of Sydney's eastern suburbs. "Mr George Collins?"

"That's what it says on the door," I said, standing and gesturing to the chair across from my desk. "Please, have a seat. You look like you could use a cup of coffee, though I should warn you it's not as good as what you're likely used to."

She moved into the room with fluid grace, settling into the chair and placing her handbag carefully in her lap. "Thank you, but no. I...I'm rather anxious about why I'm here."

I sat back down and leaned forward slightly, adopting what I hoped was a reassuring expression. "Most people who come to see me are anxious about something, Mrs..?"

"Hartwell," she said, then paused as if the name carried weight she wasn't sure she wanted to bear. "Mrs Evelyn Hartwell."

The name was familiar, though I couldn't immediately place it. Hartwell...it had the ring of money and influence, the sort of name that appeared in the business pages and society columns. I made a mental note to place it later, if need be, and focused on my potential client.

"Well then, Mrs Hartwell, what brings you to my office on this wet Thursday morning?"

She opened her handbag and withdrew a lace handkerchief, though her eyes were dry. It seemed to be more of a nervous gesture than a necessity. "Mr Collins, I've heard that you have a particular...expertise when it comes to matters involving jewellery."

I felt a familiar tingle at the base of my skull, the same sensation I used to get when casing a particularly promising mark. "It appears you know something of my background. I have some experience in that area, yes. What seems to be the problem?"

"My jewellery collection has been stolen," she said, her voice barely above a whisper. "Some of my most prized pieces. The police have been investigating for three days now, but they seem to have made no progress whatsoever."

"When did this happen?"

"Monday night. We were hosting a charity gala at our home in Point Piper—a fundraiser for the Children's Hospital. There were perhaps sixty guests, all quite respectable people from the best families in Sydney." She paused, dabbing at her nose with the handkerchief. "Sometime during the evening, someone entered our bedroom and opened our safe. They took my grandmother's diamond tiara, an emerald necklace that belonged to my mother, and a ruby bracelet that my husband gave me for our tenth wedding anniversary."

I pulled out a notepad and pencil, though I was already committing every detail to memory. In my former profession, a good memory could mean the difference between a successful job and a long stretch in Long Bay Gaol. "What's the estimated value of the stolen pieces?"

"Over ten thousand pounds," she said, and I tried not to whistle. That was more money than most working men saw in a lifetime, myself included. "The insurance company is being...difficult. They seem to think that because it happened during a party, we might have staged the theft ourselves."

"And did you?"

The question hung in the air between us like smoke from a cheap cigarette. Mrs Hartwell's blue eyes flashed with something that might have been anger, but it was gone so quickly I couldn't be sure.

"Mr Collins, I came to you because I was told you were discreet and effective. I was also told that you had a particular understanding of how thieves operate. I was not told that you would insult me within five minutes of our meeting."

I held up a hand in what I hoped was a placating gesture. "Mrs Hartwell, I apologise if I offended you. But in my line of work, I have to ask the questions that might be uncomfortable. Insurance fraud is more common than you might think, even among the best families. If I'm going to help you, I need to know everything, including whether there might be any reason someone would suspect you of staging the theft."

She was quiet for a long moment, staring out the rain-streaked window to her right. When she spoke again, her voice was softer, more vulnerable. "My husband's import business has been struggling lately. The Depression hit everyone hard, even those of us who thought we were immune. But Mr Collins, I swear to you on my mother's grave that neither my husband nor I had anything to do with this theft. Someone came into our home during what should have been a joyous occasion and violated our privacy, our security. I want them caught and punished."

There was something in her voice that convinced me she was telling the truth, at least about her own innocence. But there was also something she wasn't telling me, something that made her avoid my eyes when she spoke about her husband. In my experience, the things people didn't say were often more important than the things they did.

"When did you discover the theft? And when were the police called?"

"We discovered it the next morning, Tuesday, when I went to put away some jewellery I'd worn to the party. The safe door was closed, but when I opened it..." She shuddered slightly. "The three most valuable pieces were gone. My husband called the police immediately."

"And what did the police tell you about how the safe was opened?"

"That's what's so strange," she said, leaning forward in her chair. "The detective—Inspector Morrison, I think his name was—said there were no signs of forced entry. No scratches on the lock, no damage to the door. Whoever opened it knew the combination."

"Who else knew the combination besides you and your husband?"

"No one. At least, no one was supposed to know. We never wrote it down, never told anyone." She paused, biting her lower lip. "Although..."

"Although what?"

"Well, the safe is quite old. My husband's father installed it when he built the house thirty years ago. I suppose it's possible that someone who worked on the house might have learned the combination somehow."

I made another note. "What about your household staff? How long have they worked for you?"

"Our butler, Arthur Pemberton, has been with the family for fifteen years. He's absolutely trustworthy. Rose Murphy, our housemaid, has been with us for three years. She's a good girl, very reliable. And our cook, Mrs Patterson, has been with us for nearly eight years."

"Any recent changes in staff? Anyone new who might have had access to the house?"

Mrs Hartwell shook her head. "No, our staff has been quite stable. We treat them well and pay them fairly."

I leaned back in my chair, studying her face. She was beautiful, there was no denying that, but there was something brittle about her beauty, like fine porcelain that might crack under pressure. And there was definitely pressure here, though I wasn't sure yet what kind.

"Mrs Hartwell, I have to ask—is there anyone who might have a grudge against you or your husband? Any business rivals, former employees who were dismissed, anyone who might want to hurt you?"

For the first time since she'd entered my office, Mrs Hartwell looked genuinely uncomfortable. She shifted in her chair and her grip tightened on her handbag. "My husband's business dealings are quite complex, Mr Collins. He imports tea and silk from China, and there's always competition in that trade. But I can't think of anyone who would resort to theft."

"What about personal enemies? Social rivals?"

"We move in the best circles of Sydney society, Mr Collins. One doesn't make enemies in such circles, at least not openly." But even as she said it, I could see in her eyes that she was thinking of someone specific.

"Mrs Hartwell, if I'm going to help you, I need complete honesty. Is there someone you're thinking of?"

She was quiet for so long I thought she might not answer. Finally, she sighed and said, "There's the Weatherby family. Judge Harold Weatherby and his son Charles. There was...an unpleasant business matter between my husband and the Judge some years ago. Nothing criminal, you understand, just a dispute over import licences and trading rights. It left some bad feelings."

"Bad enough for someone to break into your house and steal your jewellery?"

"I...I don't know. I wouldn't have thought so, but..." She trailed off, staring at her hands.

"But what?"

"Charles Weatherby was at the party on Monday night. I saw him talking to several of our guests, and he seemed to know his way around the house quite well. Perhaps too well."

I made a note of the name Weatherby. In my criminal days, I'd learned that family feuds could motivate people to do things they'd never normally consider. And I'd heard of the Judge. If Charles Weatherby was familiar with the Hartwell house, he might have had opportunities to learn about the safe.

"Mrs Hartwell, what exactly do you want me to do? The police are already investigating. Why come to a private detective?"

She looked directly at me for the first time since she'd mentioned the Weatherbys, and I saw something desperate in her sapphire blue eyes. "Because the police seem more interested in proving that we staged the theft than in finding the real thief. Because I need someone who understands how criminals think and operate. And because..." She paused, then continued in a rush, "Because I'm afraid this is about more than just jewellery."

"What do you mean?"

"I think someone is trying to destroy my husband's reputation, to ruin him financially and socially. The theft happened during a charity event, Mr Collins. Half of Sydney's social elite were in our home that night. By now, everyone knows that our private safe was robbed while we were entertaining guests. People are already starting to whisper that we must have staged it for the insurance money."

I could see her point. In Sydney's tight-knit high society, reputation was everything. A suggestion of financial impropriety could destroy a man's business and social standing faster than a house fire.

"What's your husband's position on hiring me?"

"He...he doesn't know I'm here." She looked down at her hands again. "Edgar thinks we should trust the police to handle the matter. He says hiring a private detective would only make us look more guilty."

"But you disagreed."

"I can't just sit and wait while our reputation is destroyed and our belongings remain in the hands of thieves. I need to do something."

I studied her face for a moment, trying to read the emotions playing across her features. There was determination there, and desperation, but also something else —fear. She was afraid of something, and I didn't think it was just the loss of her jewellery.

"My fee is five pounds a day plus expenses," I said finally. "I'll need a retainer of twenty-five pounds to start."

Relief flooded her face. "Of course. Whatever you require." She opened her handbag and withdrew a roll of banknotes that would have been impressive even in my thieving days. She counted out twenty-five pounds and placed them on my desk.

"I'll also need a detailed description of the stolen pieces, a list of everyone who attended the party, and access to your house so I can examine the scene."

"Certainly. I have photographs of the jewellery at home, and I can provide you with the guest list." She paused. "When can you start?"

"I've already started, Mrs Hartwell. But I should warn you —if I uncover something you don't want to know, something that might be embarrassing to you or your husband, I won't stop investigating just because it makes you uncomfortable."

"I understand. I just want the truth, Mr Collins. Whatever it might be."

As she said it, I had the distinct impression that Mrs Evelyn Hartwell was lying, at least to herself. In my experience, people who said they wanted the truth usually wanted a version of the truth that didn't hurt too much. But that was her problem. My job was to find out what really happened to her jewellery, and if that led to uncomfortable revelations, so be it.

"I'll need your address and telephone number," I said, pulling out a client information form.

"We live at Bellevue Hill, Point Piper. The house is called 'Tara'—it's on the harbour with a circular drive. You can't miss it." She gave me the telephone number and I wrote it down carefully.

"One more question, Mrs Hartwell. These pieces that were stolen—were they just valuable, or did they have sentimental value as well?"

"Both," she said, and for the first time I heard genuine emotion in her voice. "The tiara belonged to my grandmother. She wore it at her wedding in 1851. The emerald necklace was my mother's favourite piece—she wore it to every important social event for twenty years. And the ruby bracelet..." She paused, touching her wrist unconsciously. "My husband gave it to me on our tenth wedding anniversary. He said the rubies matched the fire in my hair."

"So whoever took them didn't just steal valuable jewellery. They stole pieces of your family history."

"Exactly." She stood up, smoothing down her dress. "That's why I need them back, Mr Collins. The money isn't the important thing. Even our reputation isn't everything. It's what those pieces represent."

I stood as well, coming around the desk to walk her to the door. "I'll start by examining your house this afternoon, if that's convenient. I'd like to see the safe and talk to your staff."

"Of course. I'll make sure they're available to speak with you." She paused at the door, turning back to face me. "Mr Collins, may I ask you something personal?"

"You can ask. Can't guarantee I'll answer."

"Why did you give up your previous...profession...to become a private detective?"

It was a fair question, one I used to ask myself often enough. "Let's just say I discovered that there's more satisfaction in catching thieves than in being one."

She smiled for the first time since entering my office, and it transformed her face completely. "I hope you're as good at catching them as I hear you were at being one."

"So do I, Mrs Hartwell. So do I."

After she left, I sat back down at my desk and stared at the twenty-five pounds she'd given me. It was more money than I'd seen in months, and it represented the difference between paying my rent and being evicted. But more than that, it represented a case that might actually be interesting. Jewellery thefts, by their and my former nature, were a speciality of mine, of a sort, and this one had all the elements of a proper puzzle—a locked safe opened without force, valuable items stolen during a social gathering, and a client who was clearly not telling me everything she knew.

I picked up the telephone and dialed the number for police headquarters. When the desk sergeant answered, I asked to speak to Tom Majors.

"Magpie!" Tom's voice boomed through the earpiece. "Haven't heard from you in a little while. How's business?"

"Can't complain, Tom. Listen, I've just been hired to look into a jewellery theft in Point Piper. Hartwell is the name. What can you tell me about it?"

There was a pause, then Tom's voice came back in a more serious tone. "Edgar Hartwell, the importer? Yeah, we've got a file on that one. Happened Monday night during some charity do. Professional job, by the look of it. Safe was opened clean, no damage to the door or lock mechanism."

"Any suspects?"

"Nothing concrete. Could have been an inside job—someone who knew the combination and the layout of the house. Or it could have been a professional who got the combination somehow. We're still working on it."

"Mind if I take a look at the scene?"

"Would you stop if I said no?" He said with a chuckle, then sighed. "By all means. See if you can unearth something we missed. If you do, you'll let me know, right?"

"Always do. Thanks, Tom."

I hung up the phone and leaned back in my chair, thinking about what I'd learned so far. Mrs Hartwell appeared to be hiding something, that much was clear to me. Her husband didn't know she'd hired me, which suggested either that he was opposed to the idea or that she didn't trust him completely. The theft had been professional, which meant either an experienced criminal or someone with inside knowledge. And there was this business with the Weatherby family, which might be nothing or might be the key to everything.

I looked out the window at the rain, which showed no signs of letting up, and confirmed my earlier decision. I'd take the tram out to Point Piper this afternoon and have a look at the scene of the crime. The Hartwell house and its compromised safe might tell me more than Mrs Hartwell's carefully edited version of events.

But first, I checked my Longines Evidenza wrist watch. Time for an early lunch. I locked the money in my desk drawer, put on my coat and hat, and headed next door to the NSW Masonic Club. The dining room was warm and dry, filled with the comfortable smell of roast beef and tobacco smoke. I found a table by the window where I could watch the rain and think about the case while I ate.

As I waited for my meal, I thought about Mrs Evelyn Hartwell and her stolen jewellery. There was something about the case that reminded me of the old days, when I'd study a mark for weeks before making my move. The careful observation, the patient gathering of information, the gradual understanding of how all the pieces fit together. The only difference was that now I was on the other side of the law, using those same skills to catch thieves instead of being one.

The irony wasn't lost on me that my criminal past made me uniquely qualified to understand how this particular crime might have been committed. I knew how professional thieves operated, what they looked for in a target, how they gathered information and planned their moves. If the Hartwell robbery was the work of a professional, I had a better chance than most of figuring out how it was done and who did it.

But if it was an inside job, as Tom suspected, then it became a different sort of puzzle entirely. Inside jobs were messier, more personal. They involved betrayal and secrets, family dynamics and hidden resentments. They were harder to solve because the motives were often more complex than simple greed.

As I ate my steak and sipped my beer, I found myself thinking about shadows. There were shadows everywhere in this case: the shadow of Mrs Hartwell's fear, the shadow of her husband's possible financial troubles, the shadow of the Weatherby family feud, and perhaps most relevantly, the shadow of my own criminal past that qualified me to investigate the crime.

In my thieving days, I'd learned that shadows could hide important things, but they could also reveal them if you knew how to look. The angle of a shadow could tell you the time of day, the position of obstacles, the best route of escape. In detective work, I had already realised, shadows worked much the same way. The things people didn't say, the glances they avoided, the topics they changed too quickly—these shadows might be more revealing than the facts they were trying to hide.

By the time I finished my meal, the rain had lightened to a steady drizzle. I paid my bill and headed back to my office next door to collect my notebook and camera. It was time to visit the scene of the crime and see what the shadows at the Hartwell house might reveal.

As I locked up my office and headed for the tram stop, I couldn't shake the feeling that this case was going to be more complicated than a simple jewellery theft. Mrs Hartwell's nervousness, her husband's opposition to hiring a private detective, the professional nature of the job, and the timing during a social gathering all suggested layers of complexity that I was only beginning to understand.

But that was what made detective work interesting. Like my old profession, it required patience, observation, and the ability to see patterns that others missed. The only difference was that now I was using those skills in service of justice rather than personal gain.

The tram was nearly empty as it carried me through the wet streets toward Point Piper and whatever secrets the Hartwell house might be hiding. I stared out the rain-streaked windows and wondered what I would find, and whether the Hartwell family would be pleased with whatever secrets I might uncover.

~ Chapter 2 ~

The tram wound its way through the wet streets of Sydney, past the terraced houses of Paddington and up through the leafy suburbs that spoke of money and privilege. The drizzle since lunch had remained, and the grey clouds hanging over the harbour promised more rain to come. I sat near the back, watching the city change as we climbed toward the eastern suburbs. The working-class neighbourhoods with their narrow streets and washing lines gave way to broader avenues lined with jacarandas and the sort of houses that had names instead of numbers.

Point Piper was old money territory, where Sydney's merchant princes had built their mansions overlooking the harbour in the days when wool and wheat were making fortunes for those clever enough to ship them to the mills of Manchester. The houses here sat on generous blocks with harbour views that were worth more than most men earned in a lifetime. It was the sort of neighbourhood where servants still used the back entrance and where a man's social standing could be measured by the size of his grounds and the elegance of his boat shed.

I got off the tram at the junction of New South Head Road and walked the remaining distance to the Hartwell house. The address Mrs Hartwell had given me wasn't hard to find—'Tara' was exactly as she'd described it, a grand colonial revival mansion sitting on perhaps two acres of manicured grounds. The house was built in the Federation style popular thirty years ago, with wide verandahs, bay windows, and decorative fretwork that spoke of prosperity and good taste. A circular gravel drive curved up from iron gates that stood open, flanked by stone pillars topped with electric lamps that would have cost more than most men earned in a year.

I walked up the drive, my footsteps crunching on the wet gravel, and took my time studying the house and grounds. In my criminal days, I'd learned that the approach to a job was often as important as the job itself. You needed to understand the layout, the sight lines, the possible escape routes. Now I was applying those same skills from the opposite perspective, trying to understand how a thief might have operated here.

The house sat well back from the road, screened by mature gardens that would provide plenty of cover for someone who didn't want to be seen. There were several large trees close to the building—a spreading Morton Bay fig near the eastern wing and a couple of Norfolk pines that cast deep shadows even in daylight. The circular drive meant that a vehicle could approach and leave without having to reverse, always useful for a quick getaway. And the generous spacing between houses in this neighbourhood meant that screams or sounds of breaking glass were unlikely to be heard by the neighbours.

But what struck me most was how open and trusting the whole setup was. The gates weren't locked, there were no dogs that I could see, and the windows on the ground floor were large and easily accessible. It was the kind of house that had been built in a more innocent time, when the biggest security concern was keeping the servants from gossiping to the neighbours about family business.

I rang the bell and waited, listening to the sound of footsteps approaching from inside the house. The door was opened by a tall, thin man in his fifties with receding grey hair and the sort of formal bearing that marked him as a professional servant. He was impeccably dressed in a black suit with a white shirt and black tie, and his pale eyes studied me with the careful assessment of a man whose job it was to distinguish between welcome guests and unwanted intruders.

"Good afternoon," he said in a cultured voice that carried just a hint of working-class origins. "May I help you?"

"George Collins," I said, handing him one of my business cards. "Mrs Hartwell is expecting me."

He took the card and examined it carefully before stepping aside to let me enter. "Of course, Mr Collins. I'm Pemberton, the butler. Mrs Hartwell mentioned that you would be calling. Please follow me."

The interior of the house was as impressive as the exterior had promised. We entered through a spacious foyer with a parquet floor and a crystal chandelier that probably cost a fortune. The walls were panelled in dark wood and hung with oil paintings of stern-faced ancestors and pastoral scenes that spoke of European travel and expensive taste. A wide staircase curved up to the second floor, its banister polished to a mirror shine.

Pemberton led me through a series of interconnected rooms—a formal sitting room with silk wallpaper and French furniture, a library lined with leather-bound books that actually looked as if they'd been read, and finally into what was clearly the main drawing room. This was where money came to display itself: Persian rugs on polished floors, furniture that belonged in a museum, and windows that offered spectacular views of Sydney Harbour stretching away toward the bridge and the city beyond.

Mrs Hartwell was standing by one of the windows, silhouetted against the grey light from outside. She'd changed from the dark blue dress she'd worn to my office into something more casual—a light green frock that complemented her eyes and made her look younger and less formal. But the tension I'd noticed in my office was still there, visible in the way she held her shoulders and the careful way she turned to greet me.

"Mr Collins, thank you for coming so promptly." She moved away from the window and gestured to a grouping of chairs near the fireplace. "Please, sit down. Would you care for tea? Or perhaps something stronger?"

"Tea would be fine, thanks." I settled into a chair that I wasn't sure my body was good enough for and pulled out my notebook. "I'd like to start by seeing the safe, if that's possible."

"Of course. But first..." She hesitated, glancing toward the doorway where Pemberton had withdrawn to fetch the tea. "I should mention that my husband returned from his office earlier than expected. He's upstairs in his study, and he's...well, he's not entirely pleased that I've hired you."

"But he's agreed to cooperate?"

"He has little choice in the matter," she said with a slight smile that didn't reach her eyes. "I've made it clear that this is important to me."

Before I could respond, heavy footsteps echoed from the hallway, and a moment later a large man appeared in the doorway. Edgar Hartwell was the sort of man who filled a room simply by entering it—not tall, but broad-shouldered and thick through the chest, with the kind of physical presence that came from years of getting his own way through sheer force of personality. He was perhaps fifty, with iron-grey hair that was beginning to thin and a florid complexion that suggested he enjoyed his food and drink. His clothes were expensive but slightly rumpled, as if he'd been running his hands through his hair and loosening his collar.

"So you're the private detective my wife has seen fit to engage," he said without preamble, his voice carrying the flat vowels of a man who'd been born somewhere west of Parramatta but had spent thirty years trying to disguise the fact. "Edgar Hartwell." He didn't offer to shake hands.

"George Collins. I'm sorry about your loss, Mr Hartwell."

"Are you?" He moved into the room and stood with his back to the fireplace, a position that allowed him to look down at both his wife and me. "Or are you just sorry that decent people have to resort to hiring ex-criminals to get justice?"

The words hung in the air like smoke from a badly ventilated fireplace. I could feel Mrs Hartwell's embarrassment and her husband's hostility, but I'd dealt with both before. In my criminal days, I'd learned that the best response to aggression was often calm professionalism.

"Mr Hartwell, I understand your reservations about hiring me. But I've solved a lot of cases in my time and the fact is, I know how thieves think and operate because I used to be one. That knowledge might help me recover your wife's jewellery when conventional methods have failed."

"Conventional methods," he repeated with a snort. "The police have been working on this case for three days. Inspector Morrison is a competent man. He doesn't need some..." He searched for a word that wouldn't be completely insulting and settled on, "some amateur interfering with his investigation."

"Edgar, please," Mrs Hartwell said quietly. "Mr Collins comes highly recommended."

"By whom? Other criminals?"

"Police Chief Tom Majors at police headquarters recommended him to me, Edgar" Mrs Hartwell said.

I decided to chime in. "Tom Majors has known me for five years and can vouch for both my honesty and my effectiveness. If you'd prefer to check my credentials with him, I'd be happy to give you his telephone number."

The mention of Tom Majors seemed to deflate some of Hartwell's bluster. Everyone in Sydney knew Tom's reputation, and few people wanted to cross swords with him unnecessarily.

"That won't be necessary," Hartwell said grudgingly. "But I want it understood that you're working for my wife, not for me. And I expect you to coordinate with Inspector Morrison rather than conducting some sort of independent investigation that might compromise the official inquiry."

"Of course." I made a note in my book, though what I wrote was a reminder to stay well clear of Inspector Morrison until I had a better understanding of what was going on. "Now, would it be possible to examine the safe?"

Hartwell looked as if he wanted to refuse, but his wife spoke up before he could object. "Certainly. It's upstairs in our bedroom."

Pemberton reappeared with a tea service on a silver tray, but Mrs Hartwell waved him away. "We'll take tea later, Pemberton. Mr Collins would like to examine the safe first."

The butler nodded and withdrew, and Mrs Hartwell led the way upstairs with her husband following reluctantly behind. The staircase was even more impressive from the inside, with a hand-carved banister and family portraits lining the walls. I found myself looking at the faces of Edgar Hartwell's ancestors—stern men in Victorian dress and elegant women in elaborate gowns—and wondering if any of them had ever had to deal with theft or scandal.

The master bedroom was at the front of the house, with windows that looked out over the gardens and furnishings that spoke of wealth and refined taste. The bed was a massive four-poster that probably dated from the colonial period, and the walls were covered with silk wallpaper in a soft gold that complemented the heavy drapes. It was the sort of room that belonged in a museum or a very expensive hotel.

The safe was built into the wall behind a landscape painting that had been swung aside on hidden hinges. It was an old Mosler model, probably installed when the house was built, with a heavy steel door and a combination lock that looked like it hadn't been updated in decades. The door stood open, revealing empty shelves lined with green felt.

I knelt down and examined the lock mechanism carefully, using a small magnifying glass I'd brought for the purpose. In my criminal days, I'd developed a healthy respect for safes and the men who could open them. It was a specialized skill that required patience, knowledge, and a delicate touch. This particular safe was old enough that a modern professional could probably have opened it in under an hour, but it would still have required someone with experience and the right tools.

"No scratches on the metal around the lock," I observed, running my finger along the edges of the combination dial. "No drill marks or impact damage. Whoever opened this knew what they were doing."

"That's what Inspector Morrison said," Mrs Hartwell confirmed. "He seemed to think it was either someone who knew the combination or a very skilled professional."

"What was the combination?"

Edgar Hartwell hesitated, then said reluctantly, "The date we were married—tenth of June, 1916. Ten, six, sixteen."

I made a note of the numbers, though I doubted they were relevant. If the thief had known the combination, it suggested inside knowledge rather than professional safe-cracking skills.

"Who else might have known that date?"

"Anyone who knows us well," Mrs Hartwell said. "We've celebrated our anniversary every year for twenty years. It's not exactly a secret."

"But knowing your anniversary and knowing that you used it as your safe combination are two different things," I pointed out. "Was there anyone who might have observed you opening the safe?"

The Hartwells exchanged a look that told me this was a question they'd already considered and didn't like the answer to.

"The household staff, I suppose," Edgar said reluctantly. "Though I can't imagine any of them..."

"What about guests? Have you ever opened the safe while anyone else was in the room?"

"Never," Mrs Hartwell said firmly. "We're always very careful about that."

I spent a few more minutes examining the safe and the surrounding area, but there wasn't much to see. The thief had been careful and professional, leaving no obvious clues behind. I closed the safe door and swung the painting back into place, noting how smoothly the hinges operated and how completely the painting concealed the safe when closed.

"I'd like to talk to your staff now, if that's possible."

"Of course," Mrs Hartwell said. "Shall we start with Pemberton?"

We went back downstairs to the drawing room, where Mrs Hartwell rang for the butler. While we waited, I asked about the layout of the house and the movements of the staff during the party.

"The servants were all quite busy that evening," she explained. "We had sixty guests for dinner, followed by dancing in the ballroom. Pemberton was overseeing the service, Rose was helping in the kitchen and upstairs, and Mrs Patterson was managing the catering with the help of some temporary staff we'd hired for the evening."

"What time did the party end?"

"The last guests left around midnight," Edgar said. "We went to bed shortly after, exhausted from the evening."

"And you didn't check the safe that night?"

"There was no reason to," Mrs Hartwell said. "I'd put the jewellery I'd worn that night on top of the dresser there with the intention of placing it in the safe the following morning."

Pemberton appeared in the doorway, and Mrs Hartwell gestured for him to come in. "Pemberton, Mr Collins would like to ask you some questions about Monday night."

The butler nodded gravely and took a position near the door, his hands clasped behind his back in the formal posture of a man who'd spent his career in service. "Of course, sir. How may I assist you?"

I studied his face for a moment, noting the careful neutral expression and the way his eyes avoided direct contact with mine. In my criminal days, I'd learned to read people quickly —their tells, their weaknesses, their secrets. Pemberton struck me as a man with something to hide, though whether it was relevant to the theft remained to be seen.

"Tell me about Monday evening, Pemberton. Were you aware of any unusual activity in the house? Anyone going upstairs who shouldn't have been there?"

"The evening proceeded quite normally, sir. The guests arrived at seven for cocktails, dinner was served at eight, and afterward there was dancing and conversation until approximately midnight. I was supervising the service throughout the evening and noticed nothing unusual."

"Did you see any of the guests upstairs?"

"A few ladies visited the powder room on the first floor, and I believe one or two gentlemen may have stepped out onto the upstairs terrace for cigars. But that's quite normal at such gatherings."

"Do you remember who specifically went upstairs?"

Pemberton's brow furrowed in concentration. "Mrs Weatherby visited the powder room early in the evening, as did Mrs Sinclair and young Miss Foster. As for the gentlemen, I believe Mr Charles Weatherby and Dr Sinclair stepped out for cigars around ten o'clock."

I made careful notes of the names, particularly Charles Weatherby. It was interesting that he'd been upstairs during the party, and it confirmed Mrs Hartwell's earlier observation about his familiarity with the house.

"How long have you worked for the Hartwell family, Pemberton?"

"Fourteen years, sir. I came to work for Mr Edgar's father in 1921, after the war."

"And in all that time, have you ever had reason to enter the master bedroom when the family wasn't present?"

The question seemed to make him uncomfortable. He shifted slightly and his eyes flicked toward Edgar Hartwell before returning to me. "Only for cleaning purposes, sir, and then always in the presence of Rose or Mrs Hartwell herself."

"Have you ever seen the safe opened?"

"Never, sir. Mr and Mrs Hartwell are very discreet about such matters."

I asked a few more questions about the evening's schedule and the movements of the staff, but Pemberton's answers were careful and uninformative. He struck me as the sort of servant who knew exactly where his loyalties lay and wouldn't say anything that might compromise his employers, even if he suspected them of wrongdoing.

After Pemberton withdrew, I asked to speak with Rose Murphy, the housemaid. She proved to be a different sort entirely—a young woman in her early twenties with red hair and freckles who seemed nervous about being questioned by a detective. Unlike Pemberton's formal reserve, Rose had the kind of open, honest face that made lies difficult to maintain.

"I don't know nothing about no stolen jewellery, Mr Collins," she said in a broad Irish accent that spoke of recent arrival in Australia. "I was that busy Monday night, what with all the guests and the extra work."

"Tell me about your duties that evening, Rose."

"Well, I helped Mrs Patterson in the kitchen before the guests arrived, then I was upstairs most of the night, helping the ladies with their coats and making sure the powder room was tidy. Toward the end of the evening, I was clearing glasses and ashtrays from the upstairs rooms."

"Did you notice anyone acting strangely? Anyone who seemed particularly interested in parts of the house they shouldn't have been in?"

Rose bit her lower lip and glanced nervously at Mrs Hartwell. "Well, there was one thing that seemed a bit odd..."

"What was that?"

"It was that young Mr Weatherby, the judge's son. I seen him coming out of the corridor that leads to the master bedroom around half past ten. When he saw me, he seemed all flustered-like, said he'd been looking for the lavatory and got lost."

Mrs Hartwell and her husband exchanged another meaningful look. Edgar's face had darkened, and I could see he was thinking about the implications of Charles Weatherby being in the vicinity of their bedroom during the party.

"Did you believe his explanation?" I asked Rose.

"Well, sir, I thought it was peculiar, seeing as how there's a perfectly good gentlemen's lavatory downstairs, and besides, Mr Weatherby's been to the house before. He should have known where everything was."

"How many times has he been here before?"

"Oh, several times over the years, sir. The Weatherbys and the Hartwells..." She glanced nervously at her employers and trailed off.

"It's all right, Rose," Mrs Hartwell said quietly. "Mr Collins needs to know everything."

"Well, ma'am, the families used to be friendly, didn't they? Before the...unpleasantness. Mr Charles used to come to parties here regular-like, and he always seemed to know his way around quite well."

I made more notes, building a picture of Charles Weatherby as someone with both motive and opportunity. The 'unpleasantness' Rose referred to was clearly the business dispute Mrs Hartwell had mentioned, and if Charles had been a regular visitor to the house in the past, he might well have observed the safe being opened or learned about the combination through casual conversation.

After dismissing Rose, I asked to speak with Mrs Patterson, the cook. She proved to be a stout, middle-aged woman with flour-dusted hands and the no-nonsense manner of someone who'd spent her career managing kitchens and the people who worked in them.

"I don't hold with theft, Mr Collins," she said firmly when I explained why I was there. "Never have, never will. Whoever took Mrs Hartwell's jewellery ought to be strung up, and that's the truth of it."

"Were you aware of anything unusual happening Monday night?"

"The only unusual thing was how much work it was, feeding sixty people and keeping them happy. I was in the kitchen most of the night, supervising the temporary girls we'd hired for the evening. Didn't have time to notice what was going on upstairs."

"Did any of the guests visit the kitchen during the evening?"

"A few of the ladies complimented the meal, as is proper. And that Dr Sinclair came down around eleven o'clock, saying he wanted to compliment the cook personally. Charming man, very polite."

I made a note about Dr Sinclair's visit to the kitchen. It was another small detail that might or might not be significant, but in my experience, it was often the accumulation of small details that solved cases.

After finishing with the staff, I asked the Hartwells to show me the rest of the house, particularly the routes someone might have taken to reach the master bedroom unobserved. The house was large enough that there were several possible approaches, including a back staircase that the servants used and a narrow corridor that connected the main staircase to the bedroom wing.

"Someone familiar with the house could have reached your bedroom without being seen by most of the party guests," I observed.

"That's what troubles me," Edgar said grimly. "It suggests that whoever did this knew the house well."

As we completed the tour, I found myself thinking about the picture that was emerging. The theft had been carried out by someone with detailed knowledge of the house, its routines, and possibly the safe combination. The list of people with that kind of access was limited: the household staff, regular guests, and family friends who'd visited often enough to learn the layout.

Charles Weatherby fitted that profile perfectly. He'd been a regular visitor in the past, he'd been upstairs during the party at approximately the right time, and his family had a motive for wanting to hurt the Hartwells. The business dispute Mrs Hartwell had mentioned might have provided the spark, but I suspected there was more to the story than simple commercial rivalry.

"I'd like to see the guest list from Monday night," I told Mrs Hartwell as we returned to the drawing room.

She went to a writing desk and withdrew a sheet of paper covered with names written in careful copperplate. I scanned the list quickly, noting several names I recognised from the society pages of the newspapers. It was a gathering of Sydney's social and professional elite: doctors, lawyers, businessmen, and their wives. The sort of people who belonged to the right clubs, sent their children to the right schools, and would never dream of associating with anyone whose reputation was questionable, such as myself.

"Tell me about the relationship between your family and the Weatherbys," I said, settling back into my chair.

Edgar's face darkened again, and he began pacing in front of the fireplace. "Harold Weatherby is a sanctimonious hypocrite who uses his position on the bench to settle personal grudges."

"Edgar," his wife said warningly.

"It's true, Evelyn. The man has had it in for me ever since that business with the import licences."

"What exactly happened with the import licences?" I asked.

Edgar stopped pacing and stood with his back to the fireplace again, his hands clasped behind him. "Five years ago, I applied for exclusive rights to import a particular grade of tea from a supplier in Hong Kong. It was a legitimate business proposition that would have been profitable for everyone involved. But Weatherby had connections with a competing importer, and he used his influence to have my application denied."

"His influence as a judge?"

"His influence as a member of the Import Licensing Board. It's a government appointment, and judges are often asked to serve on such committees because of their supposed impartiality." Edgar's voice was bitter. "In Weatherby's case, his impartiality extended to favouring his friends and punishing his enemies."

"And you considered yourself one of his enemies?"

"I considered myself a victim of his corruption. The decision cost me thousands of pounds and nearly bankrupted my business."

I could see why there might be bad blood between the families, but I still didn't understand why Mrs Hartwell had seemed so reluctant to discuss it earlier.

"What about Charles Weatherby specifically? What's his relationship with your family?"

Mrs Hartwell answered this time, her voice carefully neutral. "Charles is...a young man with expensive tastes and limited means. His father keeps him on a very tight allowance, which doesn't always cover his social obligations."

"Gambling debts?" I guessed.

"Among other things. Charles has always been fond of high-stakes card games and horse racing. It's caused considerable tension within the family."

I was beginning to see a possible motive for Charles Weatherby. If he was short of money and harboured resentment against the Hartwells because of his father's feud with Edgar, he might have seen the theft as a way to solve both problems at once. The jewellery would provide ready cash, and embarrassing the Hartwells would be an added bonus.

"I'll need to speak with the Weatherbys," I told them. "Both the judge and his son."

"Be careful how you approach Harold," Edgar warned. "He's a vindictive man who doesn't forget slights, real or imagined. And he has enough influence in this city to cause problems for people who cross him."

"What about Charles?"

"Charles is weak," Mrs Hartwell said quietly. "He resents his father's control but lacks the backbone to break free. He might be more forthcoming if you can catch him when his father isn't around."

I made notes about the Weatherby family dynamics and added them to my growing file on the case. The picture that was emerging was one of old grudges and simmering resentments, the kind of toxic family relationships that could motivate people to acts they'd never normally consider.

As I prepared to leave, Edgar Hartwell pulled me aside for a private word. "Collins, I want you to understand something. My wife's jewellery means a great deal to her, not just financially but sentimentally. If you can recover those pieces, I'll see that you're well compensated, regardless of my initial reservations about hiring you."

"And if I uncover something you'd rather not know?"

He was quiet for a moment, staring out at the harbour where the late afternoon light was beginning to fade. "Then I suppose we'll deal with that when it happens. But understand this—I won't tolerate any scandal that might damage my business or my family's reputation. If you find evidence that someone we know socially is involved in this theft, I expect you to handle it discreetly."

It was the kind of request I'd expected from a man like Edgar Hartwell, someone who valued appearances as much as justice. But it also told me that he suspected someone in his social circle was responsible for the theft, and that he was more concerned about avoiding embarrassment than catching the thief.

As I walked back down the gravel drive toward the road, I reflected on what I'd learned during my visit to the Hartwell house. The theft had definitely been an inside job, carried out by someone with detailed knowledge of the house and possibly the safe combination. The most likely suspect was Charles Weatherby, who had motive, opportunity, and the kind of financial pressures that might drive a weak man to desperate acts.

But there were still questions that bothered me. If Charles had stolen the jewellery, how did he know the combination of the safe? Where was the jewellery now? How did he plan to dispose of pieces that were probably too distinctive to sell through normal channels? And why had he chosen to act during a party when the house was full of potential witnesses? Perhaps he realised there would also then be plenty of suspects to bedevil the police with.

The rain had started again by the time I reached the tram stop, and I pulled my coat collar up against the cold wind blowing in from the harbour. As I waited for the tram that would take me back to the city, the subject of shadows reared up again in my mind. The Hartwell house was full of them—shadows cast by old grudges, family secrets, and the kind of genteel corruption that flourished in Sydney's upper classes.

Tomorrow I would visit the Weatherbys and see what shadows their family might be hiding. But tonight, I had enough information to begin piecing together the puzzle of Mrs Hartwell's stolen jewellery and the complex web of relationships that surrounded it.

The case was shaping up to be exactly the kind of challenge I'd hoped for when I hung out my shingle as a private detective. It combined the technical aspects of a professional theft with the psychological complexity of a family drama, all set against the backdrop of Sydney's social elite and their carefully maintained facades.

As the tram carried me back through the darkening streets toward the city, I couldn't shake the feeling that I was only beginning to understand the true nature of what had happened at the Hartwell house on Monday night.

~ Chapter 3 ~

The next morning dawned grey and overcast, with the promise of more rain hanging in the air like a threat. I sat in my office on Castlereagh Street, reviewing my notes from the previous day's investigation at the Hartwell house. The case was taking shape, but there were still too many loose ends and unanswered questions for my liking.

Charles Weatherby remained my primary suspect. He had the motive—gambling debts and family resentment against Edgar Hartwell. He had the opportunity—he'd been upstairs during the party, near the master bedroom where the safe was located. And he had the knowledge—as a former regular guest at the house, he might have observed the safe being opened or learned the combination through casual conversation.

But suspicion wasn't proof, and I needed more concrete evidence before I could be certain of his guilt. More importantly, I needed to understand the man himself—his character, his desperation, and whether he was capable of the kind of professional theft that had been carried out at the Hartwell house.

By eleven o'clock, I'd made my decision. I locked up my office and walked next door to the NSW Masonic Club for an early lunch. The dining room was beginning to fill with the usual crowd of barristers, doctors, and businessmen who made up the club's membership. I found a table by the window where I could watch the street while I ate and think about my next moves.

The steak was excellent, as always, and I washed it down with a beer while reviewing what I knew so far. Charles Weatherby remained my primary suspect, but I needed more information about the other guests at Monday night's party before I could be certain. Dr Malcolm Sinclair, the surgeon who'd organised the charity gala, would be a good place to start.

After finishing my meal, I proceeded to the telephone directory lying next to the telephone in the stranger's room of the club and found Dr Sinclair's number and address there. He had a practice in Macquarie Street, near the hospital. I walked through the afternoon streets, dodging puddles from the morning's rain, and made my way to the medical district where Sydney's most prominent physicians maintained their consulting rooms.

Dr Sinclair's practice occupied the ground floor of an elegant Georgian building that spoke of professional success and social standing. The waiting room was furnished with expensive furniture and decorated with oil paintings that probably cost more than most men earned in a year, possibly more than even Dr Sinclair would ordinarily be able to afford. I presented my card to the receptionist and asked if

Dr Sinclair might spare a few minutes to discuss Monday night's charity gala.

After a brief wait, I was ushered into a consulting room where Dr Malcolm Sinclair rose from behind an imposing mahogany desk. He was tall and silver-haired, with the kind of bearing that marked him as a man accustomed to deference and respect.

"Mr Collins," he said, extending his hand, "I understand you're investigating the unfortunate incident at the Hartwell residence. How can I assist you?"

"I am indeed." I sat in the proferred chair and took a breath. "What was your impression of the evening? Did you notice anything unusual?"

"It was a typical charity gathering, really. Good food, pleasant conversation, generous donations to a worthy cause. The guests were all people I've known for years—not the sort of crowd one would associate with criminal behaviour."

"But someone at that gathering was a thief."

"Yes, well..." He seemed uncomfortable with the blunt statement. "I suppose that's the obvious conclusion. Though I must say, it's difficult to imagine any of our mutual acquaintances resorting to such behaviour."

I studied his face, noting the intelligent blue eyes and the carefully controlled expression. There was something he wasn't telling me, something that made him avoid direct eye contact when discussing the evening's events.

"Dr Sinclair, I have to ask—did you notice anyone acting strangely during the party? Anyone who seemed particularly interested in parts of the house they shouldn't have been exploring?"

His fingers drummed nervously on his desk. "Not specifically, no. Though..." He paused, seeming to wrestle with some internal debate.

"Though what?"

"Well, there was some tension in the air that evening. Nothing obvious, you understand, but the sort of undercurrents one notices when one knows the families involved."

"What sort of tension?"

"The situation between the Hartwells and the Weatherbys, primarily. Judge Weatherby and Edgar Hartwell were perfectly civil to each other, as gentlemen should be, but there was a certain...coolness in their interactions."

"And Charles Weatherby? How did he seem?"

Dr Sinclair's expression grew troubled. "Charles appeared somewhat agitated during the evening. He was drinking more than usual, and I noticed him having what seemed to be an intense conversation with several other guests. But then, Charles has been under considerable strain lately."

"What sort of strain?"

"The usual problems that affect young men of his class who lack sufficient occupation. Gambling debts, I believe, and the associated difficulties that come with such weaknesses."

I made notes as he spoke, building a picture of Charles Weatherby as a desperate young man operating under extreme pressure. "Did you speak with Charles during the evening?"

"Briefly, yes. I complimented him on his father's recent judicial appointment to the Appeals Court, and he seemed pleased by the recognition. But he excused himself rather quickly to speak with other guests."

"Do you remember who he spoke with?"

Dr Sinclair's brow furrowed in concentration. "Let me see... He had a long conversation with Mrs Foster about her daughter's coming-out party. He spoke with several of the younger men about racing and cards. And toward the end of the evening, I saw him in earnest discussion with someone I didn't recognise—a rather rough-looking individual who seemed out of place among the other guests."

This was new information, and potentially significant. "Can you describe this person?"

"Middle-aged, stockily built, with the sort of weathered complexion that comes from outdoor work. His clothes were respectable but not expensive, and he had the bearing of a tradesman rather than a professional man. I assumed he was connected to the catering staff or perhaps a driver for one of the guests."

"Did you see this man anywhere else in the house?"

"No, only in conversation with Charles in the main drawing room. But I found it odd that Charles would spend so much time talking to someone who was clearly from a different social class."

I made careful notes about the mysterious stranger. If Charles was indeed planning the theft, he might have needed help from someone with professional criminal experience. A rough-looking man who seemed out of place at a society gathering could fit that description perfectly.

"Dr Sinclair, is there anything else about the evening that struck you as unusual?"

He was quiet for a moment, staring down into his lap. When he looked up, his expression was troubled. "Mr Collins, I hope you won't take this amiss, but I feel I should warn you to be careful in your investigation of this matter. The families involved are prominent members of Sydney society, and accusations of criminal behaviour—even if ultimately proven false—can cause irreparable damage to reputations and relationships."

"Are you speaking for yourself, Doctor, or has someone asked you to deliver this warning?"

His face flushed slightly. "I'm speaking as a friend of all the families involved. Discretion is often as important as determination in matters like these."

I nodded my thanks and bade him farewell. As I walked back up Macquarie Street, I considered what I'd learned. The mysterious stranger who'd spoken with Charles Weatherby was particularly intriguing. If Charles had stolen the jewellery, he would have needed help disposing of it, and a professional fence or criminal contact would be exactly the sort of person he might have consulted.

I decided to head straight for the Weatherby house. I returned to my office and got into my car parked outside, spending the next several minutes driving to Woollahra. The sky had darkened since lunchtime, and the first drops of rain were beginning to fall as I reached the house.

The Weatherby estate was in one of the oldest and most exclusive parts of Woollahra, where colonial mansions sat behind high stone walls that spoke of old money and established social position. The house itself was built in the Victorian Gothic style, all pointed arches and decorative stonework that made it look more like a small cathedral than a family residence.

I was admitted by a middle-aged housekeeper who led me through corridors lined with family portraits to Judge Weatherby's private study. The room was dominated by a massive desk and lined with legal tomes that spoke of a lifetime spent in service to the law.

Judge Harold Weatherby was perhaps sixty-five, with white hair and pale blue eyes that seemed to miss nothing. Everything about him spoke of authority and the habit of being obeyed without question. When he looked up from the papers he'd been reading, I felt like a defendant being examined for evidence of guilt.

"Mr Collins," he said in a voice that carried the weight of thirty years on the bench, "I understand you're investigating the unfortunate incident at the Hartwell residence."

"That's correct, Your Honour. I appreciate you agreeing to see me."

"Please, sit down." He gestured to a leather chair positioned directly in front of his desk. "What exactly do you hope to learn from me?"

"I'm trying to understand the relationships between the various people who attended Monday night's charity gala. I understand that your family and the Hartwells have had some business disagreements in the past."

Something flickered in the judge's pale eyes—anger, perhaps, or calculation. "The relationship between my family and Edgar Hartwell is a matter of public record. Five years ago, I served on a government board that denied his application for certain import licences. The decision was made on purely objective grounds."

"But Mr Hartwell believes there were personal considerations involved."

"Edgar Hartwell believes many things that have no basis in fact. He's a man who confuses business setbacks with personal persecution." The judge's voice carried cold authority. "I'm afraid his tendency toward paranoid thinking has only worsened since his financial difficulties began."

"What sort of financial difficulties?"

"I'm not privy to the details of his business affairs, naturally. But it's common knowledge that the import trade has been challenging since the Depression. Many firms that seemed secure five years ago are now struggling to survive."

I made notes while he spoke, but I was more interested in his reaction when I mentioned his son. "Your Honour, I understand that Charles attended the charity gala on Monday night."

The change in the judge's demeanour was immediate and unmistakable. His pale eyes hardened, and his fingers tightened on the arms of his chair. "What does my son have to do with this investigation?"

"He was observed upstairs during the party, and I need to account for everyone's whereabouts during the relevant time period."

Judge Weatherby was quiet for a long moment, studying my face with judicial intensity. "Mr Collins, my son is a young man who sometimes exercises poor judgment. He drinks too much, gambles unwisely, and associates with people who are beneath his social station. But he is not a thief."

"Has he mentioned the theft to you? Expressed any opinions about what might have happened?"

"We've discussed it briefly. Charles was as shocked as anyone to learn of the theft. Despite the recent unpleasantness between Edgar and myself, he's known the Hartwell family since childhood."

"I understand Charles has had some financial difficulties recently."

The judge's face darkened. "My son's financial affairs are a private family matter, Mr Collins."

"Perhaps, but they might be relevant if they provided a motive for desperate action."

"Are you suggesting that my son stole Mrs Hartwell's jewellery to pay his gambling debts?"

"I'm suggesting that financial pressure can cause people to act in ways they normally wouldn't consider."

Judge Weatherby rose from his chair with controlled anger. "Mr Collins, I think this interview has come to an end.

You're welcome to speak with my son if you wish, but I won't sit here and listen to baseless speculation about his character."

"Where might I find Charles?"

"He has rooms in the city. King's Cross, I believe. He's chosen to live independently rather than remain in the family home."

The way he said it suggested that Charles's departure hadn't been entirely voluntary.

As I prepared to leave, the judge moved to the window overlooking his gardens. "Mr Collins, I want you to understand something about my son. Charles is weak, not evil. He's made poor choices, but he is not a criminal. If you're determined to pursue this investigation, please remember the difference between weakness and wickedness."

I was about to respond when footsteps echoed in the corridor outside, and a moment later a young man appeared in the doorway. He was perhaps twenty-five, with his father's pale eyes but lacking the judge's commanding presence. His clothes were expensive but slightly rumpled, and there was something nervous and furtive about his manner that immediately put me on guard.

"Father, I...oh, I'm sorry. I didn't realise you had a visitor."

"Charles," Judge Weatherby said with obvious discomfort, "this is Mr Collins, a private investigator looking into the theft at the Hartwell house."

Charles Weatherby's reaction was immediate and telling. His face went pale, and his hands began to tremble slightly. "The theft? I...I don't know anything about any theft."

"No one suggested you did," I said calmly, studying his face for signs of guilt or deception. "I'm simply trying to understand what happened during Monday night's party."

"I was there, yes. It was a charity event for the hospital. I spoke with several people, had a few drinks, left with the other guests around midnight." His voice was pitched slightly higher than normal, and he kept glancing nervously at his father.

"Did you go upstairs during the evening?"

"I...perhaps. I may have used the facilities or stepped onto the terrace for air. I don't really remember."

"You don't remember?"

"It was a social gathering, Mr Collins. I wasn't keeping a detailed log of my movements."

But there was something in his manner that suggested he remembered his movements very clearly indeed, and that he was lying about his activities upstairs.

"Mr Weatherby, I understand you've been having some financial difficulties lately."

Charles's nervous glance toward his father was answer enough, but Judge Weatherby spoke before his son could respond. "As I told you, Mr Collins, that is a private family matter."

"Of course. But I wonder if you might be able to help me with another question, Mr Weatherby. Dr Sinclair mentioned seeing you in conversation with someone he didn't recognise during the party. A middle-aged man who seemed out of place among the other guests."

Charles's face went completely white, and for a moment I thought he might faint. "I...I spoke with many people that evening. I can't recall everyone I met."

"This would have been someone who looked like a tradesman rather than a professional man. Stockily built, weathered complexion, clothes that were respectable but not expensive."

"I don't...I'm afraid I don't recall anyone matching that description."

But his eyes told a different story, and I could see that he knew exactly who I was talking about. The question was whether this mysterious stranger was connected to the theft or to some other aspect of Charles's troubled life.

Judge Weatherby had been watching our exchange with growing alarm, and now he stepped forward protectively. "Mr Collins, I think you've asked enough questions for one day. If you have specific accusations to make against my son, I suggest you present them to Inspector Morrison through proper channels."

"I'm not making accusations, Your Honour. I'm simply gathering information."

"Then I suggest you gather it elsewhere. Charles, you needn't answer any more questions without legal representation present."

As I prepared to leave, Charles suddenly spoke up, his voice barely above a whisper. "Mr Collins, you have to understand...I would never hurt Mrs Hartwell. She was always kind to me, even after the trouble between our families began. Whatever you think I might have done, I would never steal from her."

There was genuine emotion in his voice, and for a moment I saw past the nervous young man to someone who was genuinely tormented by guilt or fear. Whether that guilt was connected to the theft remained to be seen, but it was clear that Charles Weatherby was carrying a heavy burden of some kind.

"I appreciate your candour, Mr Weatherby. If you think of anything else that might be helpful to the investigation, please don't hesitate to contact me." I handed him another of my cards.

As I left the Weatherby house and walked back toward my parked car, I reflected on what I'd learned during my visit.

Charles Weatherby was clearly hiding something, and his reaction to my questions about the mysterious stranger suggested that there were aspects of this case I didn't yet understand. His emotional response to the suggestion that he might have hurt Mrs Hartwell seemed genuine, but that didn't necessarily mean he was innocent of the theft.

The rain had intensified during my visit, and by the time I made it back to my office in the city, it had become a torrential downpour. I parked my car and hurried toward my building entrance, becoming soaked even over such a short distance.

I unlocked my office door and strode inside, removing my wet coat and hung it up on the hangar to the left of my desk. I sat down and started ruminating over the complexities of the case. Charles Weatherby remained my primary suspect, but the mysterious stranger Dr Sinclair had observed added a new dimension to the investigation. If Charles had indeed stolen the jewellery, he would have needed help disposing of it, and a professional criminal contact would be exactly the sort of person he might have consulted.

But there were still questions that bothered me. Why had Charles seemed so genuinely distressed by the suggestion that he might have hurt Mrs Hartwell? And why had he been so nervous about discussing the mysterious stranger if their conversation had been innocent?

I realised that this case was becoming more complex with each new piece of information I uncovered. The shadows I was following seemed to lead not to a simple theft, but to something much more complicated and potentially dangerous.

Tomorrow I would need to track down Charles Weatherby in King's Cross and speak with him again. Perhaps confronting him about his connection to the mysterious stranger without his father close by might yield more positive results. A visit with a couple old friends might be in order as well. But tonight, I had enough new information to warrant a progress report to Mrs Hartwell.

The case was far from solved, but I was beginning to see a vague outline hidden within the shadows of Sydney's high society. Like my old profession, detective work required patience, observation, and the ability to see patterns that others missed.

~ Chapter 4 ~

The next morning brought the kind of grey Sydney dawn that makes honest men think about emigrating to Queensland. I sat in my office, nursing my second cup of black coffee and staring at the notes I'd accumulated over the past two days. The investigation was reaching a critical point where I needed to dig deeper into Sydney's criminal underworld—territory I knew well from my previous profession, but dangerous ground for a man trying to stay on the right side of the law.

Charles Weatherby's nervous reaction to my questions about the mysterious stranger suggested there were aspects of this case that went beyond simple theft. If he was involved with professional criminals, it would explain how the safe had been opened so skillfully, but it would also mean the stakes were higher than a desperate young man stealing to pay gambling debts.

I locked my office and made my way through the morning streets toward the Rocks district, where Sydney's criminal element had made their home since the first convict ships unloaded their human cargo. The narrow lanes and crumbling warehouses provided perfect cover for activities that couldn't bear the light of day, and I knew that if Charles Weatherby was dealing with professional thieves, this was where I'd find traces of their operation.

My first stop was a dingy pub called the Waterman's Arms, tucked away in a lane that most respectable citizens avoided even in daylight. The interior was thick with tobacco smoke and the kind of silence that fell over criminal haunts when strangers appeared. I ordered a beer and waited, letting my presence become familiar before I started asking questions.

Tommy Nguyen operated from a back room of the pub, dealing in goods that had changed hands without the formality of purchase. He was a thin, nervous man in his fifties who'd survived in Sydney's underworld by being useful to everyone and loyal to no one. When I finally approached him, his eyes showed recognition but no warmth.

"Magpie Collins," he said in accented English that still carried traces of his Cantonese origins. "Heard you'd gone respectable. What brings you back to the old neighbourhood?"

"Information, Tommy. I'm looking for someone who might have been moving high-end jewellery this week."

His eyes narrowed with calculation. "Official business or private?"

"Private. And profitable, if you can help me."

Tommy glanced around the pub, then gestured for me to follow him to his back room. The space was cluttered with goods of questionable provenance—watches, silverware, small antiques that had probably been 'liberated' from wealthy homes across the city.

"What sort of jewellery?" he asked, settling behind a desk that had seen better decades.

"Diamond tiara, emerald necklace, ruby bracelet. High quality, some of them antique. Would have come on the market this week."

Tommy shook his head slowly. "Nothing like that's crossed my path, Magpie. But I'll tell you what—someone's been asking around about buyers for that sort of merchandise. Didn't give his name, but he had the look of a gentleman down on his luck."

"Can you describe him?"

"Young, well-dressed but trying too hard to look casual. Nervous as a cat in a dog pound. Spoke like he'd been to university but didn't know the first thing about moving stolen goods."

It sounded like Charles Weatherby, confirming my suspicions about his involvement. But Tommy's next words surprised me.

"Thing is, Magpie, I told him I wasn't interested. Merchandise like that's too hot even for the likes of me. But I heard he might have found someone willing to take the risk."

"Who?"

"Word is he made contact with some of the boys who work the docks. Professional types who know how to move expensive items without attracting attention."

I left Tommy with a five-pound note for his information and made my way deeper into the Rocks, following leads that took me to increasingly unsavoury establishments. The dock workers Tommy had mentioned operated in a grey area between legitimate labour and outright criminality, using their access to shipping to move goods that couldn't bear official scrutiny.

By afternoon, I'd built a clearer picture of what had happened to Mrs Hartwell's jewellery. Charles Weatherby had indeed approached several fences, but his amateur approach had made most of them nervous. Finally, he'd made contact with some of the professional criminals who operated through the docks—dangerous men who wouldn't hesitate to eliminate loose ends if things went wrong.

I needed more information, and I knew where to get it. Mary 'Fingers' O'Brien ran a small antique shop in Surry Hills that served as a front for more questionable activities. She'd been my partner in crime during my thieving days, and more than that—she'd been the woman I'd planned to marry before circumstances drove us apart.

Mary's shop occupied the ground floor of a narrow terrace house, its windows displaying a carefully curated selection of genuine antiques mixed with items of more recent and dubious acquisition. The bell above the door chimed softly as I entered, and I heard her voice call from the back room.

"Be right with you!"

A moment later she appeared, and despite the many years that had passed since we'd worked together, she looked almost exactly as I remembered. Mary was thirty-two now, with auburn hair that caught the afternoon light and green eyes that seemed to see straight through to a man's soul. She'd always been beautiful, but it was a dangerous beauty that had gotten both of us into more trouble than we could handle.

"Hello, George," she said quietly, and the sound of my real name on her lips brought back memories I'd tried to forget.

"Mary. You're looking well."

"So are you. I heard you'd gone straight, become some sort of detective."

"Something like that." I glanced around the shop, noting the expensive pieces that probably hadn't come through legitimate channels. "Business seems good."

"I get by. What brings you here, George? Social call or professional business?"

"Bit of both, maybe. I'm looking into a jewellery theft, and I think the pieces might have passed through criminal channels. Something told me a young gentleman might have approached you about selling family heirlooms."

Mary's expression grew cautious. "Might have. What's your interest?"

"I'm working for the victims. They want their property back."

She moved closer, and I caught the scent of her perfume—the same fragrance she'd worn during our criminal days. "And what's in it for me if I help you?"

"Professional courtesy between old partners?"

Mary laughed, a sound that was both bitter and affectionate. "Oh, George. You always were too sentimental for your own good."

She walked to the front door and turned the sign to 'Closed', then drew the curtains across the windows. When she turned back to me, there was something predatory in her expression that I remembered all too well.

"The young man you're asking about came here three weeks ago," she said, moving closer until she was standing just inches away.

Long before the theft occurred, which told me this had been planned well in advance.

"Charles Weatherby, though he didn't give his real name. Wanted to know about selling some expensive jewellery he claimed was family pieces."

"What did you tell him?"

"I told him I wasn't interested. He had the look of someone who was going to get himself killed playing with professionals." Her hand touched my chest, fingers tracing the edge of my jacket. "But I might have mentioned that there were other people in the city who took bigger risks for bigger rewards."

"What kind of people?"

"The kind who work the docks and don't ask too many questions about where expensive goods come from." Her green eyes held mine with an intensity that made it hard to think clearly. "George, you need to be careful with this case. There are dangerous people involved, and you're not as protected as you used to be."

"Protected by what?"

"By being one of us." Her hand moved to my face, fingers tracing the line of my jaw. "Now you're on the other side, and that makes you a target if you get too close to the truth."

I should have stepped away then, should have maintained the professional distance that separated my old life from my new one. But Mary had always been my weakness, the one person who could make me forget my better judgment. When she kissed me, I found myself responding with the same desperate passion that had defined our relationship years ago.

What happened next was inevitable, I suppose. We made love with the fierce intensity of two people who knew they were playing with fire, surrounded by the shadows of stolen goods and criminal memories. Afterward, as we lay tangled together on the narrow bed in her back room, I felt the familiar mixture of satisfaction and regret that Mary had always inspired in me.

"This doesn't change anything," I said quietly.

"I know." Her fingers traced patterns on my chest. "We're still on opposite sides of the law, still too dangerous for each other. But George...be careful with this case. Whatever Charles Weatherby stole, it's brought him to the attention of people who don't forgive mistakes."

"What do you mean?"

"I mean that if he's crossed the wrong people, he might not live long enough to stand trial."

I dressed quickly, my mind already turning back to the investigation. The afternoon with Mary had been a mistake—a dangerous indulgence that could compromise everything I'd worked to build. But it had also provided valuable information about the criminal network Charles Weatherby had stumbled into.

"Mary, if you hear anything else about this case..."

"I'll let you know." She wrapped a silk robe around herself and walked me to the back door. "But George, promise me you won't try to be a hero. Some fights aren't worth winning if they get you killed."

I left through the narrow alley behind her shop, my thoughts churning with new information and old emotions. The investigation was becoming more dangerous with each new revelation, but I was committed to seeing it through. Mrs Hartwell deserved to have her jewellery returned, and justice demanded that the thief be caught and punished.

As the evening drew in, I decided to return to the Weatherby house in Woollahra. A phone call had determined Charles was likely at the family home. Mary's warnings about him being in danger had unsettled me, and I wanted to speak with him directly about his involvement with professional criminals. If he was indeed the thief, I needed to get to him before the dangerous men he'd been dealing with decided he was a liability.

The Weatherby estate looked different in the gathering dusk, its Gothic architecture casting long shadows across the manicured gardens. I approached the front door and rang the bell, but there was no answer. The house seemed strangely quiet, with no lights visible in any of the windows. Evidently nobody was home.

I walked around to the side of the house, remembering the layout from my previous visit. Judge Weatherby's study faced the garden, and I could see a dim light burning behind the heavy curtains. Something about the stillness of the scene made me uneasy, and I decided to investigate further.

The French doors leading from the study to the garden were unlocked—unusual particularly after the recent theft. I pushed them open carefully and stepped inside, calling out softly.

"Charles? Mr Weatherby?"

The study was in shadow, lit only by a single lamp on the judge's desk. But it was what I saw slumped in the leather chair behind the desk that made my blood run cold.

Charles Weatherby sat motionless, his head tilted back at an unnatural angle, his face pale and his lips tinged with blue. On the desk beside him lay a small glass vial and a hypodermic syringe, the kind used for medical injections. The sweet, cloying smell in the air told me everything I needed to know.

I approached the body carefully, checking for signs of life while being careful not to disturb the scene. Charles was dead, and had been for some little time. The syringe and vial suggested a drug overdose, but something about the scene bothered me. The young man I'd met just yesterday had been nervous and frightened, but not desperate enough for suicide.

I searched the study quickly, looking for any clues that might explain what had happened. In the desk drawer, I found evidence of Charles's gambling debts—receipts from illegal bookmakers, IOUs written in a shaking hand, and letters demanding payment in increasingly threatening terms. It was clear his father had been keeping close tabs on his son.

But it was what I found hidden behind a loose panel in the desk that made me realise the true scope of what I was dealing with. Charles had been keeping records of his attempts to sell the stolen jewellery, including names and addresses of the criminal contacts he'd approached. More disturbing still, there were notes suggesting he'd been blackmailing someone—cryptic references to 'what I saw that night' and 'the price of silence.' Odd to find such information in his father's study. One would have expected to, perhaps, find such in his King Cross digs. But here?

I stared at the body for a long moment, my mind racing with the implications of what I'd discovered. Nothing was adding up. Charles Weatherby was dead, and the timing of his death was far too convenient to be coincidental. The young man who'd been nervous and frightened just yesterday was now permanently silenced, along with whatever secrets he might have revealed about the theft.

I thought briefly about pocketing the most important documents from the desk—the records of his gambling debts and the cryptic notes about blackmail, but decided against it. Whatever Charles had known or seen, it had been dangerous enough to get him killed, and the evidence clearly planted here. For what purpose? To patsy the poor lad? To throw the authorities, including myself, off the trail? I made a mental note of some of the contents before me.

The plot had indeed thickened beyond a simple jewellery theft. Charles Weatherby's death suggested that there were far more dangerous forces at work than I'd initially realised, and that my investigation had just taken a deadly turn into something far more sinister.

~ Chapter 5 ~

I took a handerkerchief from my pocket and used it to cradle the telephone receiver in my hand. With my pen, I dialed Tom Major's number at police headquarters. The night desk sergeant answered. He sounded as weary as I expected he would look.

"Morning, Collins," he said upon my identifying myself. "You're up early, even for a private dick."

"I need to speak with Tom immediately. It's urgent."

"He's not in yet. Won't be for another hour at least I'd imagine."

"Okay, I'll call him at home then." I did so, and urged Tom and some men to get over here as quickly as possible.

The first pale light of dawn was breaking over the Weatherby estate gardens, as I took a turn there, waiting for the police to arrive but also to take stock of all that had happened. Charles was dead, and documentation left in situ to implicate him in various crimes to further enhance the appearance of suicide. It was a devious business.

In just under an hour, Tom arrived with some of his men. He looked like a man who'd been roused from much-needed sleep, but his eyes were alert and focused. I met him by the front gate.

"What have you found, Magpie?"

I gave him a detailed account of my visit to the Weatherby house, the fact that nobody appeared to be at home, describing the scene in Judge Weatherby's study, the apparent drug overdose and the dodgy evidence placed there. Tom made careful notes, occasionally asking for clarification about the position of the body and the evidence I'd observed.

"You think it was murder?" he asked when I'd finished my account.

"I think Charles Weatherby was killed because he knew something that could implicate whoever really stole Mrs Hartwell's jewellery. The timing is too convenient—he approaches criminal contacts about fencing stolen goods, and within days he's found dead of an overdose. And the evidence where it shouldn't have been. It's all too pat."

"I see what you mean. I think you're right."

"The documents planted there appear to indicate Charles was involved in more than simple theft. He may have been blackmailing someone."

"Hmm..." Tom said, rubbing his chin.

I led Tom through the gardens over to the French doors. We entered and Tom immediately moved over to examine Charles Weatherby's corpse. He examined the scene with professional thoroughness, noting the position of the syringe and the vial of morphine, the lack of signs of struggle, and the general arrangement of objects on the desk.

"It looks like suicide," he said finally, "a little too much like suicide, as you say. Let's see what the medical examiner has to say. I'll make the call."

While we waited for the coroner's team to arrive, I showed Tom the desk where I'd found the incriminating documents. We searched it together, but the loose panel had been secured and the hiding place was empty. In the time I had been outside waiting for Tom to arrive, someone had removed the evidence. To what end? This development baffled me.

"Someone's been in here," Tom observed grimly. "I know you didn't imagine those papers."

"I certainly didn't. These papers showed Charles was keeping records of his criminal contacts and notes about blackmailing someone. Someone took a hell of a risk coming in here and swiping it all while I was outside."

The sound of approaching footsteps in the corridor made us both turn toward the door. Judge Weatherby appeared in the doorway, fully dressed despite the early hour, his face grave but composed. He had been at home the whole time or he had recently returned without my knowing it. Either way, I couldn't make sense of the whole thing.

"Gentlemen," he said quietly, "I assume you're here about my son."

Tom stepped forward, his voice gentle but official. "Your Honour, I'm Police Chief Majors. I'm sorry for your loss. When did you discover the body?"

"A short time ago. I couldn't sleep, so I came down to my study to do some reading. I found Charles exactly as you see him now." The judge's voice was steady, but I could see the pain in his pale eyes. "I telephoned the police immediately. You certainly arrived in quick time."

I wasn't about to explain our presence there just yet. I studied the judge's face, looking for signs of deception. His story was plausible, but it seemed odd that he'd discovered the body so soon after I'd left the house. Either it was an unfortunate coincidence, or Judge Weatherby knew more about his son's death than he was admitting.

"Your Honour," Tom said carefully, "we need to ask you some questions about Charles's recent activities. Had he seemed troubled or depressed lately?"

The judge moved to the window, looking out at his gardens where the morning sun was beginning to burn off the overnight mist. "Charles had been under considerable strain recently. His gambling debts, his financial difficulties...I'm afraid he'd gotten involved with some very unsavoury people."

"What sort of people?"

"Bookmakers, money lenders, the kind of men who prey on weakness and desperation. Charles owed them substantial sums, and they were becoming increasingly aggressive in their collection methods."

Tom made notes while the judge spoke, but I was more interested in what he wasn't saying. There was no mention of Charles's attempts to fence stolen jewellery, no reference to his connection to the Hartwell theft. Either the judge was genuinely unaware of his son's criminal activities, or he was protecting the family reputation even in death. And he didn't mention the evidence that had been located there only a short time ago.

"Did Charles ever mention being threatened by these people?" Tom asked.

"Not directly, but he was clearly frightened. He'd been staying away from his lodgings in Kings Cross more frequently, I was told, and when he was here, he seemed constantly on edge." The judge turned back to face us, his expression pained. "I should have done more to help him, but I was too concerned about the family's reputation to take decisive action."

The medical examiner arrived with his team, and we stepped aside to let them work. Dr Pattinson was a thin, scholarly man who'd served as Sydney's chief coroner for over a decade. He examined the body with practiced efficiency, making notes about the position of the corpse and the apparent cause of death.

"Preliminary examination suggests morphine overdose," he told Tom after completing his initial assessment. "The injection site is consistent with self-administration, and there are no obvious signs of struggle or violence."

"How long has he been dead?" I asked.

"Based on rigor mortis and body temperature, I'd estimate between six and eight hours. So sometime between midnight and two in the morning."

That timeline was consistent with my visit to the house around five o'clock, but it also meant that Charles had died not long after I'd left Mary's shop. If someone had been watching my movements, they might have decided to eliminate Charles before I could speak with him again.

While the coroner's team prepared to remove the body, Tom and I proceeded upstairs to Charles's bedroom. There we found more evidence of his gambling activities—racing forms, betting slips, and correspondence with bookmakers—but nothing that directly connected him to the Hartwell theft. And not the paperwork that I had previously seen in his father's study downstairs.

"He was careful about keeping his criminal activities separate from his family life," Tom observed as we finished our search. "Smart, if he was indeed involved in the jewellery theft."

"Too smart to accidentally overdose on morphine," I replied. "Charles was desperate, but he wasn't suicidal. Someone killed him to keep him quiet. That someone then placed that evidence there to further enhance the suicide angle, then either that same somebody—or someone else—removed that evidence while I was outside waiting for you."

"It all sounds so fantastic, Magpie," Tom said, rubbing his chin again, which he often did when he was confronted with a case where he couldn't make head nor tail of the thing.

We were interrupted by the arrival of the housekeeper, a middle-aged woman named Mrs Henderson who'd worked for the Weatherby family for over twenty years. She was clearly distraught by the morning's events, but Tom questioned her gently about Charles's recent behaviour and visitors.

"He'd been very nervous lately," she confirmed, twisting her hands in her apron. "Jumping at every sound, always looking over his shoulder when he went out. And there were some rough-looking men who came to see him a few times in the past week."

"He'd been here at home then?" I asked. "Mr Weatherby said he'd been living on his own in Kings Cross for the most part."

"He was here often enough," she replied somewhat vaguely.

"Can you describe these rough-looking men, Mrs Henderson?" Tom asked.

She took a deep breath. "One was a big fellow with scarred hands and a broken nose. Looked like he'd been in plenty of fights. The other was smaller but meaner-looking, with cold eyes and expensive clothes that didn't suit his manner."

The descriptions didn't match anyone I'd encountered in my investigation so far, but they sounded like the sort of men who collected debts for illegal bookmakers. If Charles had been unable to pay what he owed, they might have decided to make an example of him.

But that still didn't explain the convenient timing of his death, or the missing documents I'd found in his father's desk. Someone with access to the house had removed evidence after I'd discovered the body, and the most likely candidate was Judge Weatherby himself.

After the body was removed and the initial investigation completed, Tom and I walked out to the garden behind the house where we could speak privately.

"What's your next move, Magpie?" he asked, lighting a cigarette and leaning against a stone wall.

"I need to follow up on those criminal contacts Charles made. Someone helped him plan the theft, and that same person might have killed him when he became a liability."

"Be careful. If Charles was murdered, you could be next on the list if you get too close to the truth."

"I'm already too close to back away now. Mrs Hartwell deserves to have her jewellery returned, and Charles deserves justice even if he was a thief."

Tom dropped his cigarette and ground it under his heel. "I'll have the lab rush the toxicology tests on Charles's blood. If there's anything unusual about the morphine or the way it was administered, we'll know within a day or two."

"And I'll keep digging into his connections with Sydney's criminal underworld. There are still pieces of this puzzle that don't fit together."

As I walked away from the Weatherby house, I reflected on how much the case had changed since Mrs Hartwell first walked into my office three days ago. What had started as a simple theft had evolved into something much more complex and dangerous, involving blackmail, organised crime, and now murder.

Charles Weatherby had been weak and desperate, but he hadn't deserved to die for his mistakes. Someone had killed him to protect a secret, and I was determined to uncover the truth regardless of the personal cost.

But first, I needed to return to my office, read through my notes and go over the entire case in my head. The journey in my car was non-eventful, and my thoughts turned to shadows, tragedy and to Mary, who was always on my mind in one way or another. She had gotten to me again, and I both resented it and reveled in it.

Back in my office on Castlereagh Street, I sat at my desk and laid my various notes out in front of me. I had the blackmail letters pretty much memorised. Thinking through the case, an interesting idea suddenly came to me. The cryptic blackmail references may have suggested the perpetrator of the theft was someone else, someone Charles had learned of and it was something worth killing to conceal. I played with this idea for some little time, but I still couldn't get all the pieces of the puzzle to fit together.

The web was indeed tightening around the truth, but I had the uncomfortable feeling that I might be walking into a trap laid by someone far more dangerous than a desperate young gambler. In the shadows of Sydney's criminal underworld, the line between hunter and hunted could shift without warning, and I needed to be prepared for whatever revelations lay ahead.

Slivers of sunlight were finally stabbing through my window into my office, but the shadows of this case seemed to grow darker with each new discovery. Charles Weatherby's death had raised the stakes dramatically, and I knew that before this investigation was over, more blood might be spilled in the pursuit of justice.

But I was committed to seeing it through, no matter where the trail led or what dangers awaited. The truth had a way of surfacing eventually, like bodies in Sydney Harbour, and I intended to be there when it finally came to light.

~ Chapter 6 ~

After several cups of coffee in my office, I decided to return to the Hartwell mansion in Point Piper. Something about Rose Murphy's nervous behaviour during my first visit had stayed with me, and Charles's death had given the case an urgency that demanded I follow every lead, no matter how tenuous.

The late morning sun was casting long shadows across the harbour as I approached the imposing facade of the Hartwell house. The same butler, Arthur Pemberton, answered the door with his usual stern efficiency, but I noticed a tension in his manner that hadn't been there before.

"I'd like to speak with Rose Murphy," I told him. "About the investigation."

Pemberton's eyes flickered with something that might have been concern. "I'm afraid Miss Murphy is no longer with us, Mr Collins. She left quite suddenly this morning, just a short time ago."

"Left? Where did she go?"

"She didn't say. Simply packed her belongings and departed without giving proper notice." His disapproval was evident in his clipped tone. "Most irregular behaviour for a member of this household."

I felt a chill of apprehension. Rose Murphy's sudden departure, coming so soon after Charles Weatherby's death, was too much of a coincidence. Either she was fleeing from something she knew, or someone had encouraged her to leave before she could reveal what she'd seen or heard.

"Did she leave any forwarding address?"

"None whatsoever. Mrs Hartwell was quite distressed by the inconvenience."

I asked to speak with Mrs Hartwell, but Pemberton informed me she was indisposed and had left instructions not to be disturbed. Something in his manner suggested he was lying, but I had no leverage to push the issue further.

As I walked back down the long driveway, I spotted a figure at the far end of the street hurrying along with a battered suitcase. Even at a distance, the slight frame and nervous gait told me this was Rose Murphy. I sprinted after her and, as I neared, called out to her.

She turned at the sound of my voice, her face pale with fear. When she saw me approaching, she glanced around frantically as if looking for an escape route.

"Miss Murphy," I said gently, "I need to speak with you about what happened at the house on Monday night."

"I can't," she whispered, clutching her suitcase tighter. "I can't talk to anyone about it. I'm ever so frightened."

"Frightened of what? What happened?"

She shook her head, tears beginning to form in her eyes. "I can't say, I just can't. I don't want no trouble."

I stepped closer, keeping my voice calm and reassuring. "Rose, I know you're frightened, but a young man is dead. Charles Weatherby was found dead this morning, and I think it's connected to what you know about the theft."

The colour drained completely from her face. "Dead? Mr Charles is dead?"

"Someone killed him to keep him quiet. If you know something about what really happened Monday night, your life could be in danger too."

For a moment she seemed ready to bolt, but then something in my expression must have convinced her I was telling the truth. She looked around nervously, then gestured toward a small café across the street.

"Not here," she said quietly. "Too many people watching."

We found a corner table in the café where Rose could sit with her back to the wall, facing the door. She ordered tea with shaking hands and spoke in whispers that barely carried across the small table.

"I heard Mr Hartwell on the telephone Monday night," she began, glancing around to make sure no one was listening. "It was after midnight, when all the guests had gone home. I was cleaning up in the kitchen when the telephone rang in his study."

"What did you hear?"

"He was angry, angrier than I'd ever heard him. He was shouting at someone about paying what was owed, about how he'd already done his part and it was time for the other person to honour their agreement."

"Did he mention any names?"

Rose nodded, her voice dropping even lower. "He said Mr Charles Weatherby's name several times. Called him a 'sniveling little blackmailer' and said he was tired of being bled dry by someone half his age. He wasn't going to pay."

The pieces were beginning to fall into place. I was now pretty sure Charles hadn't stolen the jewellery—he'd been blackmailing Edgar Hartwell about something, and the theft had likely been staged to provide Hartwell with insurance money to pay Charles off, but Hartwell had now reneged.

"What else did you hear?"

"Mr Hartwell said something about a gambling debt, about how Charles had gotten in over his head with some very dangerous people. He said if Mr Charles didn't stop demanding money, he'd let those people know where to find him. Mentioned a place called the Harbour Club."

I felt a chill as I realised the implications of what Rose was telling me. Edgar Hartwell hadn't just refused to pay Charles's blackmail demands—it appeared he'd arranged for the young man's murder by revealing his location to the criminals he owed money to. And The Harbour Club had a bad reputation as a hangout for dangerous people.

"Rose, did you hear anything about what Charles was blackmailing him about?"

She shook her head. "Not specifically. But Mr Hartwell mentioned something about 'what happened in China' and how it would ruin him if it became public knowledge."

China. Edgar Hartwell's import business dealt extensively with Chinese suppliers, and during the conversation with Dr Sinclair I'd learned about Hartwell's financial difficulties. Whatever Charles had discovered about Hartwell's business dealings was serious enough to warrant blackmail and, ultimately, murder.

"Is that why you're leaving?" I asked.

"I couldn't stay there no more, not after what I'd heard. Mr Hartwell kept looking at me like he suspected something.

Maybe he knew I'd overheard him talking. I was so frightened."

"You did the right thing."

"And I was ready to disappear, even without references," Rose said, her voice trembling. "But if Charles is really dead because of what I heard..."

"You need to tell the police everything you've told me. Police Chief Majors will protect you if you're willing to testify."

Rose stared into her teacup, weighing her options. "If I testify against Mr Hartwell, I'll never work in service again. Word gets around in our community, and no respectable family will hire someone who betrays their employer's secrets."

"And if you don't testify, Edgar Hartwell will get away with murder. And I'll certainly do what I can to find you a new position."

After a long silence, Rose nodded slowly. "All right, Mr Collins. I'll talk to your police friend. But I want protection, and I want it in writing."

I left Rose at the café with instructions to meet me at police headquarters on Phillip Street in two hours, giving me time to brief Tom about her revelations. As I walked through the morning streets back to my parked car, my mind was racing with the implications of what I'd learned.

Edgar Hartwell had stolen his wife's jewellery, but not out of financial desperation—he'd staged the theft to cover up payments to Charles Weatherby, who'd been blackmailing him about something connected to his business dealings in China. When Charles had demanded too much money, or Hartwell had simply refused to pay to the agreed amount, he had arranged for his murder by revealing his whereabouts to the dangerous criminals Charles owed gambling debts to.

But I still needed to understand what Charles had discovered that was worth killing for. Whatever 'happened in China' was serious enough to ruin Hartwell's reputation and possibly land him in prison. The answer lay in Charles's connection to Sydney's underground gambling world, particularly the exclusive Harbour Club that Rose had mentioned.

I needed to find a telephone and alert Tom to the situation, and then I decided to investigate the Harbour Club first. In the time I had before our meeting at the police station, I needed to understand the full scope of Charles's gambling activities and his connection to the criminals who'd ultimately killed him.

The Harbour Club operated out of the basement of Romano's Restaurant in Circular Quay, hidden beneath a respectable Italian eatery that served Sydney's business community. I'd heard about the club during my criminal days—it was where wealthy men went to gamble with stakes that would bankrupt ordinary citizens, and where those same men could arrange for services that weren't available through legitimate channels.

I approached the restaurant during the lunch hour, when the dining room would be busy enough to provide cover for my investigation. The maître d' was a smooth-talking Italian named Giuseppe who showed me to a table by the window without hesitation.

Over a leisurely lunch—I had skipped breakfast again—I studied the restaurant's layout and observed the staff. Several times I noticed well-dressed men being quietly escorted through a door marked 'Private' near the back of the dining room. Each time, they were accompanied by a large man who had the look of professional security.

After finishing my meal, I excused myself to use the facilities and took the opportunity to explore the back corridors of the restaurant. The 'Private' door led to a narrow staircase that descended into the basement, where I could hear the sounds of conversation and the distinctive click of gambling chips.

I was studying the staircase when a voice behind me made me freeze.

"Can I help you with something, mate?"

I turned to find myself facing a stocky man with enormous hands and the flat stare of someone who'd done violence for money. This had to be one of the security men I'd observed escorting guests to the basement.

"Just looking for the gents," I said casually. "Got turned around in these corridors."

"Gents is back that way," he said, pointing toward the main dining room. "This area's off-limits to restaurant patrons."

I nodded and began to walk back toward the dining room, but he called after me.

"Wait a minute. You look familiar. Haven't I seen you somewhere before?"

I turned back with a puzzled expression, hoping he didn't recognise me from either my criminal or now lawful days. "I don't think so. I've never been here before today."

He studied my face for a long moment, then shrugged. "Must be mistaken. But this is a private club down here, mate, invitation only. If you're interested in joining, you'll need to speak with Mr Kozlov."

Viktor Kozlov. The name rang a bell from my conversations with underworld contacts. He was a Russian émigré who'd built a reputation as someone who could arrange almost anything for the right price—gambling, women, smuggled goods, and less savoury services.

"I might be interested," I said carefully. "Gaming isn't it?"

"Exclusive gaming establishment. High-stakes poker, baccarat, roulette. The kind of place where serious men come to play serious games."

"Sounds expensive."

"If you have to ask about the stakes, you probably can't afford them." His smile didn't reach his eyes. "But Mr Kozlov is always interested in meeting new players with deep pockets."

I gave him a false name, handed him a fake business card I carried around for just such purposes, identifying myself as an investor looking for entertainment during my stay in Sydney. He studied it carefully, then nodded.

"I'll mention your interest to Mr Kozlov. If he's agreeable, someone will contact you about an invitation."

As I left the restaurant, I reflected on the dangerous game I was beginning to play. Getting inside the Harbour Club would give me access to information about Charles Weatherby's gambling debts and possibly his connection to Edgar Hartwell. But it would also put me in direct contact with the criminals who'd likely killed him.

I still had some time before my appointment with Rose Murphy and Tom Majors, time enough to return to my office and prepare for what promised to be a difficult interview. Rose's testimony would provide the evidence needed to arrest Edgar Hartwell for conspiracy in Charles's murder, but it would also make her a target for the same people who'd eliminated Charles.

The web was indeed tightening around the truth, but I was beginning to realise that Edgar Hartwell might not be the mastermind behind the conspiracy after all. He was wealthy, at least on the surface, and respectable, but he lacked the connections to arrange a professional murder. Someone else was pulling the strings, I felt sure. Someone with access to both Sydney's criminal underworld and its respectable society.

The trail was leading me deeper into dangerous territory, where the stakes were measured in lives rather than money. But I was committed to following it wherever it led, even if it meant infiltrating the very criminal organization that had killed Charles Weatherby.

The shadows were closing in from all sides, and I had the uncomfortable feeling that I was walking into a trap that had been carefully laid by someone far more dangerous than a desperate businessman trying to cover up his crimes. But sometimes the only way to catch a predator was to make yourself the prey, and I was prepared to take that risk if it meant bringing Charles's killer to justice.

~ Chapter 7 ~

The meeting with Rose Murphy and Tom Majors had gone better than I'd expected. Rose's testimony about Edgar Hartwell's telephone conversation provided crucial evidence linking him to Charles Weatherby's murder, and Tom had arranged for her protection at a safe house until the case was resolved. But I knew that testimony alone wouldn't be enough to convict Hartwell of conspiracy to commit murder. I needed concrete evidence of his criminal activities and his connection to the underworld figures who'd killed Charles.

That evidence lay in Hartwell's business records, and I knew exactly where to find them.

Edgar Hartwell's import company occupied the top three floors of a solid brick building in Bridge Street, not far from Circular Quay. I'd walked past it dozens of times over the years, also earlier today when visiting the Harbour Club. I made sure to note the building's security measures and the patterns of activity that might help me gain access after hours.

At two in the morning, the financial district was deserted except for the occasional police constable making his rounds. I approached the building from a side alley, dressed in dark clothing that would help me blend into the shadows. I also brought along a bag filled with the old tricks of my former trade. The skills I'd learned during my criminal career were proving invaluable in my new profession, though now I was breaking the law in service of justice rather than for personal gain.

The building's main entrance was well-secured, but like most commercial properties of its era, it had weaknesses that an experienced thief could exploit. A service entrance at the rear led to a loading dock where goods were delivered during business hours. The lock was substantial but not impossible, and within ten minutes I was inside the building.

I made my way up the service stairs to the third floor, where Hartwell's private office was located. The corridor was dimly lit by safety lamps, casting long shadows that reminded me uncomfortably of the moral ambiguity of my situation. I was committing a crime to solve a crime, using illegal methods to gather evidence that could save lives and bring a murderer to justice. I could live with that on my conscience.

Hartwell's office door proved more challenging than the building's entrance. The lock was modern and well-maintained, requiring delicate work with picks and tension bars. As I worked, I listened carefully for any sounds that might indicate the presence of a night watchman or security patrol.

After twenty minutes of careful manipulation, the lock finally yielded and I slipped inside the office. The room was spacious and well-appointed, with expensive furniture and oil paintings that spoke of success and respectability. But it was the large safe in the corner that drew my attention immediately.

I spent several minutes examining the safe, noting its make and model. It was a Mosler double-guard safe, probably installed when the building was constructed twenty years earlier, similar to the one in the Hartwell home. The combination lock was complex but not impossible for someone with my particular skills, though it would require patience and careful listening to detect the subtle clicks that indicated the correct numbers.

Before I worked on the safe, I searched Hartwell's desk and filing cabinets for any readily accessible documents that might provide insight into his business operations. Most of the papers were routine correspondence and contracts, but I found several items that immediately caught my attention.

In the bottom drawer of his desk, hidden beneath stacks of invoices, I discovered a leather-bound ledger that didn't match the company's official accounting books. The entries were written in Hartwell's distinctive handwriting, but they used codes and abbreviations rather than clear descriptions of transactions.

I photographed several pages of the coded ledger using a small camera I'd brought for this purpose, noting entries that corresponded to dates when Charles Weatherby might have made blackmail demands. The amounts were substantial—hundreds of pounds recorded as 'consulting fees' and 'special arrangements.'

But it was what I found in a locked drawer that truly revealed the scope of Hartwell's criminal activities. Using a thin blade to spring the simple lock, I discovered correspondence with shipping companies, customs officials, and Chinese suppliers that painted a clear picture of an elaborate smuggling operation.

The letters were carefully worded to avoid explicit references to illegal activities, but the pattern was unmistakable. Hartwell was importing goods that weren't listed on official manifests, using his legitimate tea business as cover for the operation. The nature of the contraband wasn't specified in the correspondence, but given the substantial profits indicated in the coded ledger, it was likely something far more valuable and dangerous than simple luxury goods.

I was photographing a particularly incriminating letter when I heard footsteps in the corridor outside. Moving quickly but quietly, I gathered the documents and returned them to their hiding places, then crouched behind Hartwell's desk and listened.

The footsteps stopped outside the office door, and I heard the rattle of keys. Someone was unlocking the door—either a security guard making his rounds or, worse yet, Edgar Hartwell himself working late on urgent business.

The door opened and electric lights flooded the office, temporarily blinding me after working by the dim glow of my flashlight. I heard voices—two men speaking in low, urgent tones as they entered the room.

"The books are in the safe," I heard Edgar Hartwell say, his voice tense with anxiety. "We need to destroy the evidence before the police start asking questions about the boy's death."

"Destroying evidence won't solve your problems," replied a second voice with a rough, working-class accent that I vaguely recognised—by description not from personal experience—from my visits to Sydney's criminal underworld. "Collins is getting too close to the truth, and that Murphy girl knows too much."

So Hartwell *had* known of Rose's overhearing him that night. I pressed myself closer to the floor behind and underneath the desk, trying to remain invisible while straining to hear their conversation. Through the gap beneath the desk, I could see two pairs of legs—Hartwell's expensive leather shoes and the heavy work boots of his companion.

"What do you suggest?" Hartwell asked, and I could hear the fear in his voice.

"Same thing we did with the Weatherby boy. Accidents happen to people who ask too many questions."

A chill ran down my spine as I realised I was listening to Edgar Hartwell and one of the men who'd murdered Charles Weatherby. The rough voice belonged to someone I'd heard described by witnesses but never encountered directly—a professional criminal who specialised in making problems disappear permanently.

"I never intended for Charles to die," Hartwell said, his voice barely above a whisper. "I just wanted him to stop demanding money, to leave me alone. I didn't want to pay anymore."

"He was bleeding you dry with his blackmail demands, and you knew it couldn't continue. We solved your problem efficiently and quietly."

"But now the private detective is asking questions, and that girl heard my telephone conversation. If they piece together what really happened..."

"First things first. First the evidence, then we deal with those other two snoops. We better shift our operations from the Pyrmont warehouse as well. Can't be too careful."

I heard the sound of the safe being opened. There was the rustling of papers and the clink of metal objects being moved around.

"Here's the real ledger," Hartwell said. "The one that shows the payments to Charles and the true scope of our operations."

"And the opium manifests?"

My blood ran cold as I heard confirmation of what I'd suspected. Hartwell wasn't just smuggling luxury goods—he was importing opium, probably from suppliers in China who used his tea business as a front for drug smuggling.

"Everything's here," Hartwell confirmed. "Shipping records, customs documents, payment vouchers. Enough evidence to put us both in prison for twenty years."

"Then we burn it all. Tonight."

I watched through the gap and listened as the two men began removing documents from the safe and piling them on Hartwell's desk. I couldn't see any of the paperwork from my vantage point, but I could guess as to their contents.

"What about the other stuff?"

"It's in this manila folder," Hartwell replied.

I heard further rustling, likely the folder being opened.

"The boy was cleverer than we gave him credit for," the rough voice said, no doubt examining the contents. "He managed to get pictures of our dock operations and several of our people handling the merchandise."

"He was at the docks on legitimate family business— something about his father's legal work. But he saw too much and was smart enough to recognise an opportunity."

"Smart enough to get himself killed," the other man replied coldly. "Just like anyone else who gets too curious about our business."

"My wife?" Hartwell said with a shaky voice. "She called Collins in, after all."

"Relax," ther other voice said, unconvincingly. "I'll take care of everything."

The implied threat was clear, and I realised that my own life was in immediate danger. If these men discovered me hiding in the office, I wouldn't live to see the morning. But I also knew that the evidence they were about to destroy was crucial to proving Edgar Hartwell's guilt and bringing Charles's murderers to justice.

I knew my current position was extremely precarious. Hartwell would only have to move to sit at his desk and my being there would be exposed. I had to act quickly and decisively. As the two men continued sorting through the safe, their backs turned to me, I carefully moved from behind the desk toward the office door, staying low and using the furniture for cover. My goal was to reach the corridor and escape the building before they knew someone had been listening to their conversation.

But as I reached the door, I accidentally knocked over a small wastepaper basket, sending it clattering across the floor. The noise was slight, but in the quiet office it sounded as loud as a gunshot.

Both men turned toward the sound, and I found myself staring into the cold eyes of Jimmy "The Hammer" Morrison —the same enforcer I'd heard about during my investigation of Sydney's criminal underworld. He was exactly as described: stocky and powerful, with scarred hands and the flat, emotionless stare of a professional killer. The hands also matched the description of one of the men seen with Charles by the Weatherby housekeeper.

"Well, well," Morrison said, his hand moving inside his jacket toward what was undoubtedly a weapon. "It looks like our private detective problem just walked right into our hands."

Edgar Hartwell's face went pale as he recognised me. "Collins! What are you doing here?"

I straightened up slowly, keeping my hands visible and my voice steady. "Learning the truth about Charles Weatherby's murder and your smuggling operation, Mr Hartwell."

Morrison stepped forward, his hand now gripping the handle of a gun concealed beneath his jacket. "You've learned too much for your own good, Collins. Just like the Weatherby boy."

"The police know I'm here," I lied, hoping to buy time or make them hesitate. "If I don't return by morning, they'll come looking for me."

Morrison laughed, a sound completely devoid of humor. "I very much doubt that, but in any event, we have plenty of time. You're going to have an unfortunate accident, just like Charles did."

I glanced around the office, looking for anything that might serve as a weapon or provide an escape route. The window behind Hartwell's desk faced the street, but we were three stories up and the building lacked any kind of fire escape. The door I'd entered through was now blocked by Morrison, and his companion was moving to cut off any other avenue of retreat.

"Before you kill me," I said, playing for time, "I'd like to understand what Charles discovered that was worth murdering him for. Professional curiosity."

Hartwell looked like he was about to be sick, but Morrison seemed almost pleased to have an audience for his confession.

"The boy stumbled onto our operation by accident," he said. "He was at the docks on some legal business for his father and saw our people unloading a special shipment. Got curious and started taking pictures with a little camera he carried."

"Pictures of what?"

"Our dock workers handling cases marked as tea but filled with premium opium from our Chinese suppliers. One of the crates had fallen and spilled its valuable contents. High-quality stuff worth more than most people see in a lifetime. The Weatherby boy got it all on camera."

The pieces were finally falling into place. Charles had discovered Hartwell's drug smuggling operation and used the evidence to blackmail him. When the demands became too expensive and threatening, Hartwell had used his criminal connections to arrange Charles's murder.

"How did you make it look like an overdose?" I asked.

Morrison smiled coldly. "Easy enough when you know the right people. We grabbed the boy from his rooms in King's Cross, took him back to his father's house, and injected him with pure morphine. Left the syringe and vial to make it look like suicide from gambling pressure. Left some material there to strengthen our case."

"And his father never suspected?"

"The judge saw what he wanted to see—a weak son who couldn't handle his debts and took the coward's way out."

I felt a surge of anger at the casual way Morrison described Charles's murder, but I forced myself to remain calm. Getting emotional would only give him an excuse to kill me sooner rather than later.

"What about Rose Murphy? Are you planning to kill her too?"

Hartwell spoke up, his voice shaking. "That wasn't part of the plan. I knew she'd overheard my conversation. I was thankful she up and left of her own accord."

"You were weak in letting her go without any consequence," Morrison said grimly. "I had people tailing her. I knew of your meeting with her at police headquarters. Which means she's a liability we can't afford to ignore any longer."

The cold calculation in his voice made it clear that Rose's life was in immediate danger, even ensconced in the safe house as she currently was, along with my own. I had to find a way to escape and warn Tom Majors about the threat to his witness.

But first, I needed to survive the next few minutes.

Morrison had drawn his gun and was pointing it directly at my chest. "Any last words, shamus?"

I raised my hands higher and took a cautious half-step back. Morrison's revolver never wavered.

"You're making a mistake," I said, my voice calm. "You kill me here, and someone else will just pick up where I left off. The evidence, the girl, the photographs—they're all out there. You can't scrub it all clean."

"Watch me," Morrison said, thumb easing back the hammer.

That's when the telephone on Hartwell's desk rang. A harsh, jarring sound in the silence.

Morrison flinched—just slightly—but it was enough. I moved.

I grabbed the heavy brass lamp from the nearby sideboard and hurled it directly at the desk light above us. The bulb shattered in a flash, plunging the room into sudden darkness. Morrison fired—once, twice—the muzzle flare lighting the room for an instant. I threw myself sideways, hitting the floor hard behind a leather armchair.

"Get the lights back on!" Hartwell shouted.

But I was already moving, crawling low, fast. My hand found the umbrella stand near the door. I yanked out the heaviest one—oak, thick and knobbed—and rose as Morrison turned toward the sound.

I brought it down hard across his gun hand. The revolver clattered to the floor, and Morrison let out a grunt of pain. I didn't wait. I drove the tip of the umbrella into his stomach, forcing him back toward Hartwell, who stumbled into a chair.

I bolted for the door, snatching Morrison's revolver as I passed. Gun in hand, I ran down the corridor and into the stairwell, taking the steps two at a time, not stopping until I hit the street.

The cool early morning air hit me like a slap. My chest heaved as I glanced up at the office windows. Lights flickered back on.

They wouldn't follow. Not yet. They needed time to recover—and more importantly, to destroy the evidence they hadn't yet touched. They'd be heading for the warehouse in Pyrmont. So would I.

I hurried to where I'd left my parked car. I was a deft hand at tailing suspects, but they'd likely be expecting me to do exactly that. Still, at this juncture, I had no other alternative. I had to see the case through.

I watched from the shadows across the street as Morrison and Hartwell exited the building fifteen minutes later. Morrison was holding a satchel, Hartwell carried nothing. They climbed into a black Studebaker parked under a streetlamp and drove off.

I rechecked the revolver in my pocket, then adjusted my coat collar before cautiously following them in my car.

This wasn't over.

Not by a long shot.

~ Chapter 8 ~

The warehouse district of Pyrmont was a labyrinth of shadows and industrial decay, where legitimate commerce mixed uneasily with less savory enterprises. I'd followed Edgar Hartwell and Jimmy Morrison here after my escape, staying far enough behind to normally avoid detection while keeping their car in sight through the narrow streets. I knew, though, that in this situation, they would know I'd be right behind them.

They'd parked outside a nondescript brick building near the wharves, where the smell of coal smoke and harbour water hung heavy in the night air. I positioned myself behind a stack of shipping crates across the street, watching as Morrison produced a set of keys and unlocked a side entrance to the warehouse.

From my hiding place, I could see light spilling from the building's high windows as they moved through the interior.

This warehouse was the likely location of their opium shipment, which Morrison had indicated they might now be moving elsewhere, but perhaps there was other evidence here that could be disposed of in much quicker fashion.

After twenty minutes of observation, I decided to risk a closer look. The warehouse sat at the end of a dead-end street, with loading docks facing the harbour and a maze of smaller buildings providing cover for my approach. I made my way carefully through the shadows, happy to still be wearing the dark clothing I had chosen for my earlier infiltration of the Hartwell offices.

The side door Morrison had used was locked, but a loading dock at the rear of the building offered better possibilities. The large doors were secured with a heavy chain and padlock, but a smaller personnel door nearby showed signs of frequent use. The lock was substantial but not impossible, and after several minutes of careful work with picks and tension bars, I gained entry to the warehouse.

The interior was dimly lit by electric bulbs hanging from the ceiling, casting pools of yellow light between vast areas of shadow. The space was filled with wooden crates and burlap sacks arranged in neat rows, all bearing the distinctive markings of Hartwell's import company. But it was the activity in the center of the warehouse that made my blood run cold.

A dozen Chinese workers were carefully opening crates marked as tea shipments, removing smaller packages wrapped in oiled cloth from hidden compartments within the legitimate cargo. The packages were being sorted and repackaged into different containers, while Morrison supervised the operation with the casual efficiency of someone who'd done this many times before. Even so, he appeared to be in something of a rush.

Edgar Hartwell stood to one side, nervously checking his pocket watch and occasionally wiping perspiration from his forehead despite the cold night air. He looked like a man who'd gotten in far deeper than he'd ever intended, trapped by circumstances beyond his control.

I positioned myself behind a stack of empty crates where I could observe the operation while remaining hidden. From this vantage point, I could see that the packages being removed from the tea crates contained a dark, sticky substance that had the unmistakable appearance of raw opium.

While I had known of all this since my earlier encounter with Morrison and Hartwell in the latter's office, the scope of the operation was nevertheless staggering to see. Hundreds of pounds of the drug were being processed through what appeared to be a regular shipment of legitimate tea. This clearly was an established smuggling network that had been operating for months or more likely years.

Morrison moved through the workers with the authority of someone who understood every aspect of the operation. He checked the quality of the opium, counted packages, and made notes in a small ledger that he kept in his jacket pocket. This wasn't just muscle work for him—he was a key organiser in the smuggling network.

"How much longer?" Hartwell asked nervously, approaching Morrison with obvious reluctance.

"Another hour to pack up this shipment," Morrison replied without looking up from his ledger. "We need to get outta here before that shamus arrives."

"Collins? He doesn't know the location of this warehouse?" Hartwell said nervously.

"He likely tailed us here, though I didn't notice anyone when I looked. We might have gotten lucky and lost him, but I don't want to risk anything. Not with this much at stake."

I felt some sense of satisfaction in Morrison's not noticing my presence in following them there. Still, they were aware of my intentions, which made my current predicament all the more dangerous.

Carefully, I removed the small camera I still had with me and began photographing the warehouse operation. The workers, the opium packages, Morrison's supervision, and Hartwell's nervous presence all needed to be documented if I hoped to bring down the entire network.

"The Chinese suppliers are getting impatient too," Morrison continued. "They want assurance that their shipments will continue to move through the docks without interference. If we can't guarantee that, they'll find other partners."

"What does all that mean?"

"We have to eliminate anyone who threatens the operation. That means Collins, the Murphy girl, and anyone else who might testify about what they've seen or heard."

Hartwell's face went pale. "You're talking about multiple murders. My wife?"

"I'm talking about protecting a business arrangement that's worth thousands of pounds per month," Morrison replied harshly, ignoring the comment about Hartwell's wife. "This operation has made you wealthy, Edgar, and it's kept your legitimate business afloat during difficult times. If you're not prepared to do what's necessary to protect it, perhaps you should consider withdrawing from the partnership."

The threat in Morrison's voice was unmistakable. Edgar Hartwell wasn't just a partner in this operation—he was trapped by it, unable to withdraw without facing consequences that might prove fatal.

I continued photographing the operation while straining to hear every word of their conversation. The evidence I was gathering would be crucial for prosecution, but I also needed to understand the full scope of the network and identify all the participants.

"I never meant any of this to happen," Hartwell said in a low sob. "I didn't want anyone to die. I just needed the money to keep us afloat. I just wanted Charles to stop bleeding me dry."

"The mistake you made was letting him live after the first demand," Morrison continued. "You should have had him eliminated immediately, before his actions could bring other people into the situation."

"I thought if I paid him initially, he would—"

"And I told you that was impossible," Morrison said sharply, cutting him off. "Blackmailers never disappear—they just come back with bigger demands until you're completely under their control."

The warehouse operation was winding down as the workers finished repackaging the opium and preparing it for distribution elsewhere. I watched as Morrison distributed small payments to each worker, noting their faces for future identification. These weren't hardened criminals but desperate men willing to risk imprisonment for wages that probably seemed generous compared to their other options.

"Where is all this headed?" Hartwell asked.

"I've got a backup location arranged in Woolloomooloo, closer to the docks and with better escape routes if the police come calling. But it's going to cost more, and our Chinese partners want additional guarantees about security. I can't blame them after what happened with that Weatherby boy."

I made careful note of this latest information. Such intelligence would be crucial for intercepting future shipments and dismantling the entire network.

As the workers began cleaning up and preparing to leave, I realised my opportunity for gathering evidence was coming to an end. But I'd seen and heard enough to understand the full scope of the operation and the dangers it presented to society.

Morrison was more than just an enforcer—he was a key organiser who understood every aspect of the smuggling network. Edgar Hartwell was a reluctant partner who'd become trapped by his own greed and fear. The operation was sophisticated, profitable, and ruthless in eliminating threats.

I was preparing to make my exit when disaster struck. As I shifted position to get a better angle for photographing one last bit of evidence, my foot caught the edge of a loose board, sending it clattering across the warehouse floor.

The sound echoed through the building like a gunshot, and every person in the warehouse turned toward my hiding place. For a moment that seemed to last forever, nobody moved.

Then Morrison's hand went inside his jacket, and I knew he was reaching for another weapon.

"We've got company," he announced calmly, his voice carrying clearly across the warehouse. "That shamus is here somewhere."

I cursed my misfortune. I had perhaps ten seconds before they reached my position. The personnel door I'd entered through was forty yards away, across open floor with no cover. The loading dock was closer but heavily secured. My only option was to create confusion and try to escape in the chaos.

I grabbed one of the empty crates and hurled it toward the electric lights, plunging a section of the warehouse into darkness. In the confusion that followed, I heard Morrison shouting orders to his men while Hartwell's voice rose in panic.

"Find him!" Morrison commanded. "Shoot him on sight. He knows everything!"

I moved quickly through the darkened area, using the maze of crates and equipment for cover while making my way toward the loading dock. Behind me, I could hear footsteps and voices as Morrison's men spread out to search the warehouse.

The loading dock doors were chained shut, but the mechanism for opening them was accessible from inside. I began working frantically to release the chains while listening for approaching footsteps.

"He's over here!" someone shouted, and I heard running footsteps approaching my position.

The chains finally gave way, and I managed to raise one of the loading dock doors just enough to crawl underneath. I found myself on a wooden platform that extended over the harbour, with the dark water lapping at the pilings below.

"There he goes!" Morrison's voice echoed from inside the warehouse. "Don't let him reach the street!"

I heard the personnel door slam open as Morrison's men rushed outside to cut off my escape routes. But they'd made the mistake of assuming I would try to reach dry land and safety.

Instead, I dove from the loading dock into the cold winter waters of Sydney Harbour.

The shock of the water took my breath away, and for a moment I struggled to orient myself in the darkness. The harbour was deeper here than I'd expected, and the current was stronger than it appeared from the surface.

I heard voices and saw flashlight beams sweeping the water as Morrison's men searched for me from the dock. But the darkness and the maze of pier pilings provided cover as I swam away from the warehouse, staying underwater as much as possible to avoid detection.

The swim to safety was the longest of my life. My waterlogged clothes weighed me down, and the cold sapped my strength with every stroke. But desperation gave me endurance, and after what felt like hours, I reached a public wharf several blocks from the warehouse.

I hauled myself out of the water and collapsed on the wooden planking, shivering and exhausted but alive. In the distance, I could see lights still moving around the warehouse as Morrison's men continued their search.

The camera I'd used to document the operation was sadly ruined by the harbour water, but the images I'd captured were burned into my memory. I'd witnessed Edgar Hartwell's opium smuggling operation, heard Morrison's earlier confession about murdering Charles Weatherby, and learned about the network of corruption that made the operation possible.

But I'd also made myself a target for elimination. Morrison confessed everything to me when he thought he had me in his power, now knew I'd seen their operation and would testify about their criminal activities at the first opportunity. He wouldn't rest until I was silenced permanently, just like Charles Weatherby. Likewise for Rose Murphy and even, possibly, Mrs Hartwell.

As I made my way slowly back to my parked car, I realised the case had taken an even deadlier turn. What had begun as a simple jewellery theft had uncovered a sophisticated criminal network that reached into the highest levels of Sydney society.

The web was indeed tightening, but I was no longer sure whether I was the hunter or the hunted in this dangerous game. All I knew was that the evidence I'd gathered tonight would either bring down a murderous criminal organization or get me killed in the attempt.

The price of silence in this case was measured in human lives, and Charles Weatherby had already paid the ultimate cost for threatening to expose the truth. Now it was my turn to decide whether justice was worth risking everything, including my own life.

The shadows were closing in from all directions, but I was committed to seeing this investigation through to its conclusion, no matter how dangerous the path ahead might prove to be.

~ Chapter 9 ~

Dawn was breaking over Sydney as I made my way back to my office, my clothes still damp from the harbour water and my mind reeling from what I'd witnessed at the Hartwell building and the Pyrmont warehouse. The evidence I'd seen and heard was damning—Edgar Hartwell was running a sophisticated opium smuggling operation, and Jimmy Morrison had confessed to murdering Charles Weatherby to protect their criminal enterprise.

But I knew that testimony alone wouldn't be enough to convict them. With my camera ruined, I needed more than my word against theirs, and I needed to understand the full scope of Charles's involvement in the case. Was he just a simple blackmailer, or was there more to it than just that? A gut feeling was beginning to tell me it was the latter, but the key to everything lay with Judge Harold Weatherby, and it was time to confront him with the truth about his son's activities.

I changed into dry clothes I had on-hand in my office and fortified myself with strong coffee before making the journey to Woollahra. The Weatherby estate looked different in the morning light—less imposing and more melancholy, as if the weight of recent tragedy had settled over the grounds like a shroud.

The same elderly housekeeper answered the door, her face drawn with grief and exhaustion. She led me to the judge's study, where I found Harold Weatherby sitting behind his massive desk, staring at a framed photograph of his son.

"Mr Collins," he said without looking up. "I wondered when you'd return. Inspector Morrison has concluded his investigation into Charles's death. He's ruled it an accidental overdose brought on by the stress of his gambling debts."

"Judge Weatherby, I'm afraid he's wrong on that score, and Police Chief Majors will back that up. Your son was murdered, and I have evidence to prove it."

He finally looked up, his eyes red-rimmed with grief and sleepless nights. "Murdered? That's impossible. Charles died alone in his room, and there were no signs of violence."

"There were no signs of a struggle because Charles was killed by professionals who knew how to make murder look like an accident." I pulled out a chair and sat down across from his desk. "Your son was blackmailing Edgar Hartwell about an opium smuggling operation, and when the demands became too expensive, Hartwell arranged for Charles's elimination."

The judge's face went white. "Blackmail? Charles wouldn't...he wasn't capable of such a thing."

"I'm afraid he was, Judge. And I think you suspected as much, even if you didn't want to admit it to yourself. You found the paperwork here by your son's body and removed it, didn't you?"

For a long moment, Harold Weatherby stared at the photograph on his desk. He finally nodded and when he at last spoke, his voice was barely above a whisper.

"Charles came to see me three weeks before he died. He was excited about something, claimed he'd found a way to solve all his financial problems without asking me for another penny. When I pressed him for details, he became evasive, said it was a business opportunity that required discretion."

"Did you believe him?"

"I wanted to. God help me, I wanted to believe my son had finally found the motivation to make something of himself." The judge's voice cracked with emotion. "But Charles had never shown any aptitude for legitimate business. His only talents seemed to be gambling and disappointing the people who loved him."

I leaned forward in my chair. "What else did he tell you about this business opportunity?"

"He mentioned something about photographs—said he'd stumbled onto information that certain prominent citizens wouldn't want made public. At the time, I assumed he was talking about some society scandal or extramarital affair."

"But you suspected it was more serious than that."

Judge Weatherby nodded slowly. "Charles had always been observant, even as a child. He noticed things that others missed, remembered details that seemed insignificant to everyone else. If he'd discovered something genuinely damaging about Edgar Hartwell's business practices..."

"He had, Judge. Your son discovered that Hartwell was smuggling opium through his legitimate tea import business.

Charles photographed the operation and used the evidence to extort money from Hartwell."

The judge closed his eyes as if the words caused him physical pain. "My son was a blackmailer."

"He was a young man drowning in gambling debts who saw what he thought was an easy solution to his problems. But he underestimated the ruthlessness of the people he was dealing with. Perhaps he thought he could outsmart them."

"Tell me how he died," the judge said quietly. "I need to know the truth, no matter how painful."

I described what I'd learned the night before, what Morrison had told me and what I had witnessed at the warehouse. Morrison's casual confession about grabbing Charles from his rooms, taking him to his father's house, and injecting him with pure morphine to make it appear like suicide from gambling pressure hit the judge like a piledriver.

"They chose your house because it provided a plausible narrative," I explained. "A weak son who couldn't handle his debts and took the coward's way out. They knew you'd see what you expected to see—Charles finally succumbing to the weaknesses that had plagued him all his life."

The judge was silent for several minutes, processing the horrible truth about his son's death. When he finally spoke, his voice had regained some of its judicial authority.

"What evidence do you have to support these accusations?"

"You saw some of the evidence here for yourself the night you discovered your son's body. And, as I said, I witnessed the smuggling operation firsthand and heard Morrison confess to the murder. But my camera was damaged in my escape. I realise my testimony alone won't be enough to convict them. I need corroborating evidence, and I need to understand exactly how Charles discovered Hartwell's activities. What was he doing down by the docks with his camera?"

Judge Weatherby stood and walked to a filing cabinet in the corner of his study. He removed a thick folder and placed it on the desk between us.

"Charles was helping me research some old cases involving shipping disputes at the docks. It was make-work, really—an attempt to give him some legitimate employment and keep him away from the gambling halls."

I opened the folder and found dozens of legal documents related to customs violations, shipping manifests, and import licensing disputes dating back several years. Many of the cases involved Edgar Hartwell's company.

"Charles was supposed to verify shipping records at the docks and cross-reference them with customs documents," the judge continued. "He was actually quite good at the detail work, better than I'd expected. But he started asking questions about discrepancies he'd noticed."

"What kind of discrepancies?"

"Shipments that appeared on dock manifests but not on customs declarations. Containers that were listed as one weight when they arrived but showed different weights when they left the warehouse. Charles thought it indicated systematic corruption among dock workers and customs officials."

I studied the documents, noting Charles's handwritten notes in the margins. His observations were meticulous and damning—he'd identified patterns that clearly indicated smuggling activities above and beyond the smashed crate— and its contents—that he had photographed.

"Did you take his concerns seriously?"

The judge's face flushed with shame. "I dismissed them as the overactive imagination of a young man looking for excitement. Charles had a history of wild theories and conspiracy thinking. I assumed he was seeing criminal activity where none existed."

"But he persisted in his investigation."

"Against my direct orders. I told him to focus on the legitimate legal research and stop chasing shadows. But Charles had always been stubborn when something captured his interest. And he was certainly stubborn when it came to anything I ever told him to do."

I found a sheet of paper covered with Charles's handwriting—dates, times, and detailed observations of nighttime activities at specific warehouse locations. At the bottom of the page, he'd written Edgar Hartwell's name followed by several question marks.

"This is how he discovered the operation," I said, showing the judge his son's notes. "Charles was conducting surveillance of the docks during his legitimate research and noticed the pattern of after-hours activity at Hartwell's warehouses."

"And he was intelligent enough to realise what he was seeing."

"More than that—he was resourceful enough to document it with photographs. Morrison told me one of the crates had fallen and shattered, revealing its ugly contents. Charles took pictures of it all. He wasn't just a dissolute gambler, Judge. He was a bright young man who might have made something significant of his life if he hadn't gotten involved with the wrong people."

The judge took the paper and read his son's notes, his hands trembling slightly. "Charles always had potential. Even as a child, he could see connections that others missed, solve puzzles that frustrated adults. But he lacked discipline and sound judgment."

"The gambling debts made him desperate, and desperation led him to make choices that ultimately cost him his life. From my experience, blackmail never ends well."

"What can I do to help bring his killers to justice?"

I gathered up the documents and returned them to the folder. "These research notes provide crucial evidence of how Charles discovered the smuggling operation. Combined with testimony from Rose Murphy about Hartwell's threatening phone call, we have the foundation for a murder case."

"But you need more."

"I need to prove further the connection between Hartwell's smuggling operation and Charles's murder. And I need to identify all the participants in the criminal network, including the corrupt officials who made the operation possible."

Judge Weatherby walked to the window and stared out at his meticulously maintained gardens. "Charles loved this house when he was young. He used to play detective games in the garden, pretending to solve mysterious crimes and catch dangerous criminals."

"In a way, that's exactly what he was doing when he discovered Hartwell's operation."

"And it got him killed." The judge turned back to face me, his expression hardening with resolve. "Mr Collins, I want you to know that I'll do everything in my power to help you bring these men to justice. Charles may have been a blackmailer, but he didn't deserve to die for it."

"There's something else you should know, Judge. Mrs Hartwell was genuinely unaware of her husband's criminal activities. Her distress about the jewellery theft was real, and she's as much a victim in this case as anyone else. And her life could now be at risk as well."

"Edgar always was skilled at maintaining appearances. His family's reputation in Sydney society is spotless, and his business practices appeared completely legitimate."

"That respectability was exactly what made him valuable to the smuggling network. No one would suspect a prominent businessman like him of trafficking in illegal drugs."

"Be careful, Mr Collins. These people have already killed once to protect their operation. They won't hesitate to kill again if they feel threatened."

"I understand the risks, Judge. But your son deserves justice, and the people of Sydney deserve to be protected from the criminals who are poisoning our community with their poison."

As I prepared to leave, Judge Weatherby handed me a small photograph of Charles as a young boy, smiling and confident in his school uniform.

"That's how I want to remember him," the judge said quietly. "Before the gambling and the debts and the poor choices that led to his death. Charles was capable of great things, Mr Collins. Don't let his mistakes overshadow the fact that he was fundamentally a good person who got in over his head. Weakness is not a mortal sin."

I pocketed the photograph and shook the judge's hand. "I'll do everything I can to make sure his killers are brought to justice."

As I walked back toward my car, I reflected on the tragic waste of Charles Weatherby's life. He'd been a bright young man with real potential who'd allowed gambling debts to lead him down a path that ultimately cost him his life.

But he'd also been brave enough to investigate criminal activity and resourceful enough to document evidence that could bring down a dangerous smuggling network. His death had been senseless and brutal, but his research would prove crucial in achieving justice.

The case was becoming clearer, but it was also becoming more dangerous. Edgar Hartwell and Jimmy Morrison knew I was onto their entire operation, and they'd already demonstrated their willingness to kill anyone who threatened their criminal enterprise.

The next phase of my investigation would require infiltrating the corrupt network that made the smuggling operation possible. I needed to identify the dock workers, customs officials, and other participants who'd been bribed to look the other way.

But first, I had to survive long enough to gather that evidence and present it to the authorities. Morrison's men were undoubtedly searching for me throughout Sydney, and my narrow escape from the warehouse had only bought me temporary safety.

The web was tightening around the truth, but the predators caught in that web were fighting back with increasing desperation and violence. The next few days would determine whether justice would prevail or whether Charles Weatherby's murder would remain officially unsolved, buried beneath the respectability and corruption that made such crimes possible.

~ Chapter 10 ~

The pieces of the puzzle were beginning to form a disturbing pattern, but I needed to understand how Edgar Hartwell had assembled such a sophisticated network of corrupt officials. The answer came to me as I sat in a café at the far end of Macquarie Street, for I dared not return to my office or home until this business was resolved.

Among Charles's research notes, I found references to several men whose names had appeared in multiple shipping disputes—Dennis Fletcher, a customs inspector; Robert Manning, a dock supervisor; and Dr Malcolm Sinclair, who had organised the charity gala where the fake jewellery theft had taken place. What connected these men to Edgar Hartwell wasn't immediately obvious, but something about the pattern nagged at my memory.

It wasn't until a waitress delivered my lunch that I rememebered a previous lunch I had taken at the NSW

Masonic Club, my usual digs, where I had overheard a conversation at the next table about an upcoming lodge meeting. The speaker mentioned several names that I now recognised from Charles's research—Fletcher, Manning, and Sinclair were all members of the same masonic lodge as Edgar Hartwell.

The realisation hit me like a physical blow. Hartwell hadn't randomly assembled his network of corrupt officials— he'd recruited them from within the masonic brotherhood, using the bonds of lodge membership to ensure loyalty and secrecy. The very institution that was supposed to promote moral virtue and mutual support had been corrupted into a criminal conspiracy.

I finished my meal quickly and decided to risk a trip to the club. Located next door to my office building, the risk to my safety was thus blatantly obvious, but I felt I had to take that risk all the same. I made my way up Macquarie Street, past the hospital, on the way to the club's location in Castlereagh Street. With my hat pulled low and the collar of my coat drawn high, I made my way down a side alley round to the back of the building and entered through a service entrance. Once inside, I quickly strode to the club's library, where membership records and lodge directories were kept for reference. As someone with full admittance to the club's facilities—I'd done the club secretary a good turn once and was granted lifelong access as a result—I was able to get to these documents, though I'd never had reason to consult them before.

The records confirmed my suspicions. Edgar Hartwell, Dennis Fletcher, Robert Manning, and Dr Malcolm Sinclair were all members of St. Andrew's Lodge No. 195, one of Sydney's oldest and most prestigious masonic lodges. They'd been initiated within a few years of each other and had served together on various lodge committees.

But it was the meeting minutes from the past year that revealed the true scope of their conspiracy. Hidden within routine business discussions about charitable activities and lodge maintenance were coded references to "special projects" and "mutual assistance arrangements" that clearly referred to the smuggling operation.

The minutes showed that lodge meetings had been used to coordinate the timing of shipments, discuss security concerns, and distribute payments to participants. Dr Sinclair's medical knowledge had been particularly valuable—not just for murdering Charles Weatherby, but for treating injuries sustained by dock workers during the dangerous work of handling smuggled goods.

I photographed the most incriminating pages of the lodge records with my spare camera, noting dates that corresponded to major shipments identified in Charles's research. The pattern was unmistakable—the masonic lodge had been transformed into a criminal organization that used ritual and tradition to mask illegal activities.

As I worked through the documents, I began to understand how Dr Sinclair fit into the conspiracy. His role in organising the charity gala hadn't been coincidental—it had provided the perfect cover for staging the fake jewellery theft. With a houseful of potential suspects and social obligations that would keep Edgar Hartwell visible throughout the evening, the doctor had helped create an unshakeable alibi for his fellow lodge member.

But Sinclair's involvement went deeper than providing alibis. The meeting minutes referenced his 'special medical services' in connection with the 'Chinese arrangements'—a coded reference to his role in Charles's murder. The doctor had used his medical knowledge to inject Charles with a fatal dose of morphine, ensuring the death appeared to be an accidental overdose rather than murder.

The charity gala itself had been carefully chosen for the fake theft. Dr Sinclair had insisted on holding the fundraiser at the Hartwell mansion, ostensibly because of their elegant ballroom and harbour views. But the real reason was to provide Edgar with an ironclad alibi while the 'theft' was being staged.

I found correspondence between Sinclair and Hartwell discussing the details of the gala, including specific mentions of timing and security arrangements. The letters were carefully worded to avoid explicit references to criminal activity, but the underlying conspiracy was clear to anyone who understood the context.

The scope of the masonic lodge's corruption was breathtaking. What had begun as a business arrangement between Edgar Hartwell and his Chinese suppliers had evolved into a comprehensive criminal network that included customs officials, dock supervisors, and medical professionals. The bonds of brotherhood had been perverted into bonds of criminal conspiracy.

Dennis Fletcher's role as customs inspector had been crucial to the operation's success. His position gave him access to shipping manifests and inspection schedules, allowing the conspirators to time their activities to avoid detection. The lodge records showed regular payments to Fletcher, disguised as 'charitable contributions' and 'lodge assessments.'

Robert Manning's position as dock supervisor had provided similar advantages. He could ensure that specific warehouses were available for nighttime operations and that dock workers asked no questions about unusual cargo. His payments were recorded as *'consulting fees'* for lodge construction projects that existed only on paper.

The criminal network had operated with remarkable efficiency, using the respectability of masonic membership to deflect suspicion and the ritual secrecy of lodge meetings to coordinate illegal activities. No outsider would question why prominent businessmen and professionals met regularly in private, and the tradition of masonic discretion provided perfect cover for criminal planning.

But it was Dr Sinclair's involvement in Charles's murder that demonstrated how completely the lodge's moral foundations had been corrupted. The doctor had taken an oath to preserve life and promote healing, yet he'd used his medical knowledge to commit murder in service of the criminal conspiracy.

I found detailed notes in Sinclair's handwriting describing the effects of morphine overdoses and the techniques needed to inject the drug without leaving obvious evidence of murder. The notes were hidden within routine medical journals in the lodge library, disguised as academic research but clearly intended as planning documents for Charles's elimination.

The charity gala had provided more than just an alibi for Edgar Hartwell—it had served as a final planning meeting for Charles's murder. Under the cover of social conversation and charitable activities, the conspirators had finalized the details of their plan to eliminate the young blackmailer.

Dr Sinclair had volunteered to handle the medical aspects of the murder, using his access to pure morphine and his knowledge of injection techniques to ensure Charles's death appeared accidental. The timing had been carefully coordinated to coincide with the fake jewellery theft, creating a complex web of deception that was designed to confuse investigators and provide multiple alibis.

As I reviewed the evidence I'd gathered, I realised the masonic lodge connection explained several puzzling aspects of the case. The sophisticated coordination between different participants, the careful timing of various criminal activities, and the remarkable loyalty that had kept the conspiracy secret all made sense when viewed through the lens of lodge membership.

The conspirators weren't just business partners—they were sworn brothers who had pledged to support each other through ritual and tradition. That brotherhood had been corrupted into criminal conspiracy, but it remained powerful enough to ensure absolute loyalty and secrecy.

I was preparing to leave the club library when I heard footsteps in the corridor outside. While it could easily have been just an innocent club member either intent on conducting research or perhaps placing new documentation into the archives, the possibility also existed it could be someone connected to the case. I couldn't risk it being the latter.

Quickly, I returned the lodge records to their proper places and gathered up my camera and notes. But as I moved toward the library's main entrance, I heard voices that made my blood run cold.

"Collins was sighted in this vicinity" Jimmy Morrison's cold and harsh voice was easily recognisable.

"We can't afford to let him piece together the lodge connection," the harried voice of Edgar Hartwell responded.

I realised I was trapped in the library with the two men who'd already murdered Charles Weatherby, and who had also tried to murder me, now approaching. The main entrance was blocked by their presence in the corridor, and the library's only other exit was a window that faced a three-storey drop to the street below.

Moving carefully to avoid making noise, I positioned myself behind the card catalogs where I could observe the entrance while remaining hidden. Through the gap between the wooden drawers, I watched as Hartwell and Morrison entered the library.

"He was here," Morrison said, examining the table where I'd been working, though there was no evidence of my having been there left extant. "I can feel that damn shamus' presence."

"He knows everything, he could destroy us all" Hartwell said nervously.

"If he's been here, if he's read these lodge records, photographed them—"

"We'll all hang for Charles's murder, for everything," Hartwell finished.

Morrison nodded grimly. "Which is why Collins has to be found. He dies tonight. No more accidents or overdoses—this needs to look like a robbery gone wrong or a random act of violence. Every day he remains alive increases the risk that he'll expose our entire network."

"What about Dr Sinclair? He's becoming unreliable, asking too many questions about our future plans."

"The doctor—and that Murphy girl—will be handled after we deal with Collins. Anyone who threatens the operation gets eliminated—no exceptions."

I listened in horror as the two men planned multiple murders to protect their criminal enterprise. The masonic lodge that was supposed to promote virtue and brotherhood had become a haven for killers who viewed human life as an expendable commodity.

"Collins has to be dealt with tonight," Morrison continued. "And we need to get back to the Harbour Club and plan it all."

The Harbour Club. The mention of that vile den raised the hairs on the back of my neck. Was that establishment more involved in this criminal operation than I had previously thought? As I pondered that question, the two men continued their discussion, and I realised my investigation had uncovered something far more than just a case of blackmail or even murder. The corruption of St. Andrew's Lodge represented a fundamental betrayal of everything masonic principles were supposed to represent— honesty, integrity, and mutual support in lawful endeavors.

Instead, the lodge had become a criminal organization that used ritual and tradition to mask murder, drug smuggling, and systematic corruption. The bonds of brotherhood had been perverted into bonds of criminal conspiracy, and the secrecy that was meant to protect lodge traditions had been used to conceal evidence of serious crimes.

Dr Sinclair had violated his medical oath by using his knowledge to commit murder. Dennis Fletcher had betrayed his public trust as a customs inspector. Robert Manning had corrupted his position as dock supervisor. And Edgar Hartwell had used his business reputation to provide cover for drug trafficking.

But it was the systematic way they'd corrupted the masonic lodge that made their crimes particularly heinous. They'd taken an institution dedicated to moral improvement and mutual support and transformed it into a criminal conspiracy that threatened the very fabric of Sydney society.

As Morrison and Hartwell left the library, I remained hidden behind the card catalogs, processing the full implications of what I'd discovered. The evidence I'd gathered would be enough to destroy not just the criminal conspiracy but the reputation of St. Andrew's Lodge itself.

The masonic connection explained everything—the loyalty between conspirators, the sophisticated coordination of criminal activities, and the remarkable secrecy that had protected the operation for so long. But it also made my investigation far more dangerous, because I was now threatening not just individual criminals but an entire network of corrupt officials who had everything to lose.

The web of conspiracy reached deeper into Sydney society than I'd imagined, and the men caught in that web were prepared to commit any crime necessary to protect their secrets. Charles Weatherby had died because he'd threatened to expose their operation, and now they were planning to eliminate anyone else who posed a similar threat.

The shadows were closing in from all directions, but I was more determined than ever to see justice done. The corruption of masonic principles made their crimes even more reprehensible, and the people of Sydney deserved to know how their most trusted institutions had been perverted to serve criminal ends.

~ Chapter 11 ~

After my near-discovery at the club, I knew time was running out. If found, Morrison and Hartwell were planning to eliminate me that very night, and I needed to gather the final pieces of evidence before they could strike. I almost had the entire pieces of the puzzle put together, but there remained one last portion before I could conclude the case. I had to return to the Harbour Club to confirm the connections between the gambling operation and the smuggling network that Morrison's words seemed to indicate.

The rain had started again that late afternoon as I made my way through the city streets, using every trick I'd learned during both my criminal career and my life as a private detective to avoid being followed. Morrison's men would be watching my office and my usual haunts, but they might not expect me to walk directly into their territory. Or so I hoped.

Romano's Restaurant was busy with the dinner crowd when I arrived, providing perfect cover for my infiltration of the basement gambling operation. This time, I wasn't trying to gather intelligence through careful observation—I needed to force a confrontation that would reveal the final connections in the criminal network.

Giuseppe, the maître d', recognised me immediately and led me to the same table I'd occupied during my previous visit. But as I studied the dining room, I noticed several men who had the hard look of professional security. Morrison had anticipated my return and prepared a trap.

"Mr Collins," a familiar voice said behind me. "Mr Kozlov would like to speak with you downstairs."

I turned to find the stocky security man who'd questioned me during my first visit to the restaurant. This time, he knew my real name and his hand rested casually on something concealed beneath his jacket. He smiled wickedly at me.

"I'm flattered by the invitation," I replied, keeping my voice steady. "But I'm quite comfortable here in the restaurant."

"I'm afraid Mr Kozlov insists. He has some questions about your interest in our establishment and your connections to certain recent events."

The threat was unmistakable. I could either accompany him voluntarily to the basement gambling operation, or his associates would ensure my compliance through less pleasant means. Around the dining room, I noticed other hard-faced men positioning themselves to block potential escape routes.

"In that case, I'd be delighted to meet Mr Kozlov," I said, rising from my chair with calculated calm.

The stocky security man led me through the now-familiar route to the basement staircase, his hand never straying far from his concealed weapon. As we descended into the Harbour Club, I could hear the sounds of gambling and conversation that masked whatever confrontation awaited me below.

The basement was more crowded than even I expected, with well-dressed men gathered around gaming tables while attractive women served drinks and provided companionship. But the atmosphere felt off somehow—more tense and watchful, as if everyone was waiting for something to happen.

Viktor Kozlov, as I came to know, sat at a corner table that provided clear sightlines to every entrance and exit. He was smaller than I'd expected, with thinning hair and expensive clothes that couldn't quite disguise his working-class origins. But his eyes held the cold calculation of a man who'd survived in dangerous circumstances through careful planning and ruthless execution.

"Mr Collins," he said in accented English, gesturing for me to take the chair across from him. "Please, sit. We have much to discuss."

I settled into the indicated chair, noting that Kozlov's security men had positioned themselves around the room in a pattern that would prevent any attempt at escape. Whatever conversation we were about to have, I wouldn't be leaving unless Kozlov was satisfied with the outcome.

"You've been asking questions about Charles Weatherby," Kozlov continued, pouring himself a measure of vodka from an expensive bottle. "Questions that suggest you know more about recent events than would be healthy for a private detective."

"Charles was murdered," I said directly. "And I believe his death was connected to gambling debts he owed to your establishment."

Kozlov smiled, but the expression held no warmth. "Charles Weatherby was a weak young man who got in over his head with debts he couldn't pay. When desperate people make poor choices, unfortunate consequences sometimes follow."

"You're talking about blackmail."

"I'm talking about a foolish boy who thought he could solve his problems by threatening people far more dangerous than himself." Kozlov's voice hardened. "Charles discovered certain business arrangements that were meant to remain private. Instead of taking a generous payment to forget what he'd seen, he decided to strike out on his own, thinking he could make more money to escape his servitude to me."

The pieces were falling into place. Charles hadn't just stumbled onto Hartwell's smuggling operation while working for his father—he'd been directed to it through his gambling connections at the Harbour Club. Kozlov and his associates had been using Charles's legitimate access to the docks as a way to gather intelligence about shipping security and customs procedures. It was far more than just a simple blackmailing case gone wrong. As I had surmised, it was far more than that.

"You were using Charles to scout the docks for weaknesses in your smuggling operation," I said.

"Charles needed money to pay his gambling debts, and we needed someone with legitimate reasons to be at the docks during business hours. It was a mutually beneficial arrangement—until Charles saw too much and became greedy."

"And when he demanded more money than you were willing to pay?"

Kozlov's expression darkened. "Charles took things into his own hands. Thought he could make more money from Hartwell than from me."

I felt a chill as I realised the full scope of the conspiracy, and the error in my initial investigation. The Harbour Club wasn't just a gambling establishment—it was the central coordinating point for the entire criminal network. Kozlov—the true mastermind behind everything, not Morrison—had been using his position to recruit assets like Charles while providing a meeting place for the corrupt officials involved in the smuggling operation.

"Edgar Hartwell was a regular customer here?" I asked, fishing for confirmation.

"Mr Hartwell appreciated our discretion and the quality of our clientele. Many respectable businessmen found our establishment useful for conducting certain types of negotiations."

"Negotiations about smuggling opium through legitimate tea imports."

Kozlov's hand moved slightly toward his jacket, and I realised I was pushing too hard too fast. Around the room, his security men had subtly shifted position to close off any escape routes.

"You already seem to know just about everything, Mr Collins. I don't feel I need to say anything more."

"I've been investigating a murder, Mr Kozlov," I pressed. "Charles Weatherby was killed because he threatened to expose your operation."

"Charles Weatherby died because he made poor choices and associated with dangerous people. Sometimes the consequences of such choices prove fatal."

The casual way Kozlov discussed Charles's murder made it clear he'd been directly involved in planning—ordering—the young man's death. But I needed him to reveal more details about the network's operations and the connections between the various participants.

"Dr Malcolm Sinclair was also a customer here," I said, taking another calculated risk.

Kozlov's eyes narrowed. "The good doctor appreciated our medical discretion when certain business associates required treatment for injuries sustained during their work. Industrial accidents can be quite serious when not properly managed."

The idea that Sinclair hadn't just provided medical services for Charles's murder—he'd been treating injuries sustained by dock workers and smugglers during their dangerous activities—had now been confirmed. The Harbour Club had served as an unofficial medical facility where gunshot wounds and other suspicious injuries could be treated without official documentation.

"And Dennis Fletcher? Robert Manning? Were they customers too?"

"Many public servants find our establishment useful for relaxation after dealing with the stresses of their positions. We provide a private environment where they can discuss their professional concerns without fear of oversight."

The pattern I suspected was now crystal clear. Kozlov had systematically recruited corrupt officials by providing them with gambling opportunities, entertainment, and a secure meeting place. Once they were compromised by their association with illegal gambling, he'd gradually drawn them into the larger smuggling conspiracy. Morrison, far from being the ringleader, was likely Kozlov's chief lieutenant, the one responsible for seeing the day-to-day operations of the business through, and the one responsible for tying up any unfortunate loose ends. Charles Weatherby was one such loose end. I was proving to be another.

"You've built quite an extensive network," I said.

"Successful businesses require careful relationship management and attention to the needs of valued clients. We simply provide services that aren't available through more conventional establishments."

As we talked, I noticed increased activity around the gaming tables. Men were quietly settling their accounts and preparing to leave, while staff members began cleaning up with unusual efficiency. The Harbour Club was being shut down for some reason. And I began to fear I knew what that reason was.

"I'm afraid our conversation will have to come to an end now, Mr Collins," Kozlov said, checking an expensive pocket watch. "We have other business to conduct this evening, and your presence creates certain complications."

"What kind of complications?"

"The kind that require permanent solutions." Kozlov's smile returned, but this time it was genuinely menacing. "You've learned too much about our operations, and you've demonstrated a troubling inability to be dealt with using our usual...methods."

I realised the trap had been sprung. Morrison and Hartwell, the former seemingly aware of my presence in the masonic club library as they spoke, had lured me to the Harbour Club knowing that Kozlov would handle my elimination in an environment completely under their control. The basement gambling operation was the perfect location for a murder that could be disguised as a robbery or random violence. Or, even more likely, I would simply disappear without a trace, no one knowing of my having been here or where I had gone.

"Edgar Hartwell is afraid you're going to eliminate his wife," I said, hoping to buy time by revealing information that might concern Kozlov. "Mrs Hartwell might have become suspicious of her husband's activities and represents a threat to your entire operation."

Kozlov's expression didn't change. "If that is the case, then I trust my associates to deal with the situation as they see fit."

"Morrison?"

Kozlov merely nodded. "I have the utmost confidence in his ability to manage all aspects of our business dealings."

The cold calculation in Kozlov's voice made it clear that Mrs Hartwell's life meant nothing to him. She was simply another potential witness who might need to be eliminated to protect the criminal conspiracy.

"You're talking about murdering an innocent woman."

"It's all just business to me. Nothing is ever personal. Individual concerns must sometimes be subordinated to larger considerations."

As Kozlov spoke, I noticed his security men moving closer to our table. The other patrons had cleared out of the basement, leaving only the criminal leadership and their enforcers. Whatever they planned to do to me, they wanted privacy and complete control over the environment.

"Before you kill me," I said, playing for time, "I'd like to understand how you recruited Charles in the first place. Professional curiosity."

Kozlov seemed amused by the request. "Charles was drowning in gambling debts and desperate for any solution to his problems. We simply offered him a way to earn money using skills and access he already possessed."

"You mean his legitimate reasons for being at the docks."

"We've been through all this already, Mr Collins. Your stalling for time won't work, I assure you."

The sound of footsteps on the basement stairs interrupted our conversation. Morrison appeared at the bottom of the staircase, his hand resting on the grip of a gun concealed beneath his jacket.

"Time to go, Collins," he said coldly. "We have business to discuss in an even more private spot."

I realised this was my last chance to escape before being taken to whichever room Morrison planned to eliminate me. A facility such as this likely had multiple storage rooms, and I remembered there was a loading dock at the rear and likely a service entrance somewhere. If I could create enough confusion to reach one of those alternate routes...

"Actually," I said, rising slowly from my chair, "I think I'll stay here and continue my conversation with Mr Kozlov."

Morrison's gun appeared in his hand with practiced efficiency. "I wasn't making a request."

"Neither was I," I replied, and threw my chair at the nearest gaming table.

The crash of the chair against the table and the scattering gambling equipment created the chaos I needed. As Kozlov's men rushed toward the disturbance, I rolled behind an overturned roulette wheel and scrambled toward the storage rooms at the back of the basement.

Behind me, I heard Kozlov shouting orders while gun shots echoed through the confined space. Bullets splintered the wooden walls around me as I reached a storage room door and dove through the opening.

I was in luck. The storage room I had entered connected to a service corridor that ran the length of the building's basement level. I could hear footsteps and voices as Kozlov and Morrison's men spread out to search for me, but the maze of storage rooms and utility spaces provided temporary cover.

My goal was the service exit I'd spotted during my previous reconnaissance of the exterior of the building. If I could then reach the harbour-side loading docks, I might be able to escape through the maze of businesses and shipping facilities that surrounded the restaurant.

But as I made my way through the basement corridors, I realised Kozlov's men knew the building's layout better than I did. They were systematically checking each room and cutting off potential escape routes with the efficiency of professionals who'd planned for this contingency.

Despite this, I managed to reach the service exit, which was locked from the inside. A few moments of work with my picks gained me access to the loading dock area. The harbour air felt cold after the close atmosphere of the basement, and the sound of water lapping against the dock pilings provided cover for my movements.

Behind me, I heard the service door slam open as Morrison's and others of Kozlov's men reached the loading dock. But the darkness and the maze of shipping containers provided cover as I made my way toward the street level and relative safety.

The chase through the warehouse district reminded me of my escape from the Pyrmont operation, but this time I was better prepared for the pursuit. I knew Morrison's men would expect me to head directly for police protection or my own office, so I chose a more circuitous route that would take me through areas where I could find temporary shelter.

As I finally reached the relative safety of the main commercial district, I knew the confrontation at the Harbour Club had provided the final confirmation I needed. Kozlov was the central coordinator of the criminal network—the true ringleader behind the whole enterprise—using his gambling operation to recruit corrupt officials and coordinate smuggling activities.

But I'd also confirmed what had been previously hinted at by Morrison, that Mrs Hartwell was in immediate danger, and I had to act quickly to warn her before Morrison and his associates could eliminate another witness to their crimes.

The cat and mouse game was entering its final phase, but the predators were becoming increasingly desperate and dangerous. The next few hours would determine whether justice would prevail or whether the criminal conspiracy would succeed in eliminating everyone who threatened their profitable empire of corruption and violence.

~ Chapter 12 ~

My escape from the Harbour Club had bought me temporary safety, but I knew Kozlov's warning about Mrs Hartwell wasn't an idle threat. If he and Morrison had decided she posed too great a risk to the operation, she would be eliminated as efficiently and brutally as Charles Weatherby had been, no matter what Edgar Hartwell might say about the matter. He was clearly in no position to argue.

I made my way through the darkening streets toward Point Piper, initially using every precaution to avoid the surveillance network that Kozlov and Morrison had undoubtedly deployed throughout the city, then took a taxi the remainder of the way. The evening fog was rolling in from the harbour, providing additional cover as I reached and approached the Hartwell mansion.

The house looked different yet again as I approached through the landscaped grounds. Most of the windows were dark, and there were no signs of the usual domestic activity that characterised a wealthy household. The silence felt ominous, as if the building itself was holding its breath in anticipation of violence.

I circled the property carefully, noting that Edgar Hartwell's automobile was absent from its usual place in the circular driveway. But there were signs of recent disturbance— tire tracks in the gravel that suggested vehicles had left in haste, and a side door that stood slightly ajar despite the evening's cool temperature.

Deciding to enter via a different vantage point, I used my picks to gain entry through a servants' entrance and moved carefully through the darkened corridors. The house felt abandoned, but I could somehow sense that something violent had occurred recently. Furniture in the main hall was disturbed, and I noticed what appeared to be scuff marks on the polished floor, confirming my initial intuition.

In the drawing room I found clear evidence of a struggle. A lamp was overturned, papers were scattered across the carpet, and there were signs that someone had been dragged from the room toward the rear of the house.

Arthur Pemberton, the butler, lay unconscious behind the overturned sofa, a large bruise visible on his temple. He was alive but deeply stunned, and my attempts to revive him produced only incoherent mumbling about 'men with guns' and 'taking her to the boat.'

The boat! When looking into Edgar Hartwell at the start of this case, I discovered he owned a private yacht that he moored in Rose Bay, using it for entertaining business associates and weekend excursions. If Morrison and his cohorts were planning to eliminate Hartwell's wife, the yacht would provide the perfect location—isolated, private, and with easy access to the deep waters of Sydney Harbour where a body might never be recovered.

I left Pemberton with a glass of water and clear instructions to contact Tom Majors as soon as he felt fully able. Then I made my way quickly toward Rose Bay, knowing that every minute of delay increased the likelihood that Mrs Hartwell would share Charles Weatherby's fate.

The Rose Bay marina was shrouded in fog when I arrived in my car, the forest of masts and rigging creating ghostly silhouettes in the dim light from the harbour-side street lamps. I could hear the sound of engines somewhere in the distance, suggesting that boats were moving despite the poor visibility.

The harbourmaster's office was closed for the evening, but I could see lights on several of the larger yachts moored in the marina's most expensive berths. The Hartwell yacht, *Southern Cross*, was berthed at the end of the main pier, and I could see activity on her deck despite the late hour.

As I inched my way carefully along the pier, staying in the shadows cast by other boats, I could hear voices carrying across the water. Edgar Hartwell's distinctive tone was unmistakable, but there was a quality of desperation in his voice that suggested events were spiraling beyond his control.

"This is madness, Morrison," Hartwell was saying as I crept closer to the yacht. "Evelyn doesn't know anything concrete about our arrangements. Killing her will only create more problems."

"She knows enough to destroy us all if she talks to the police," Morrison's rough voice replied. "And after tonight's problems with Collins, his escaping, we cannot afford any further loose ends."

I positioned myself behind a nearby sailboat where I could observe the *Southern Cross* without being seen. Through the yacht's cabin windows, I could see Mrs Hartwell tied to a chair, her face pale with terror but her posture defiant. Morrison stood over her with a gun while Edgar paced nervously around the cabin.

"The plan is simple," Morrison continued. "We take the yacht out into the harbour, make it look like a robbery gone wrong, and dump the body where it won't be found. By morning, you'll be a grieving widower with a perfect alibi."

"I tell you we can't do this," Hartwell said in a pleading tone. "And what about Collins? He's still out there, gathering evidence against us."

"He's got all the evidence already. We'll handle him soon enough, rest assured. He can't hide from us forever. He'll need to return to his office or home eventually. And when he does, we'll have him. But first, we clean up this immediate problem."

I realised I had perhaps ten minutes before they would take the yacht out into the harbour, where any rescue attempt would become infinitely more dangerous, if not impossible. I needed to act quickly and decisively, but Morrison was armed and undoubtedly prepared for trouble.

The marina's small boat rental facility was located near the pier's entrance, and I remembered seeing several motorboats tied up there during my approach. If I could commandeer one of those boats, I might be able to intercept the yacht or at least follow it into the harbour.

Working quickly but quietly, I selected a small but powerful motorboat that I was sure would be fast enough to keep pace with the larger yacht. The engine started on the third pull, but the sound carried clearly across the water in the still night air.

On the *Southern Cross*, I saw Morrison appear on deck, scanning the marina for the source of the engine noise.

Unfortunately, he spotted my boat almost immediately and began shouting orders to someone inside the cabin.

The yacht's engines roared to life, and I could see Edgar Hartwell frantically casting off the mooring lines while Morrison kept his gun trained on Mrs Hartwell in the cabin. They were preparing to make a run for the open harbour, where the fog and darkness would provide cover for what they planned to do.

I gunned the motorboat's engine and gave chase as the *Southern Cross* pulled away from the marina. The larger yacht had more power, but my smaller boat was more maneuverable and could take risks that the expensive yacht couldn't afford.

The chase led us out into the main channel of Sydney Harbour, where the fog was thickest and the landmarks were obscured by the murky conditions. I could barely make out the yacht's stern lights ahead of me, but I could hear the sound of her engines echoing off the harbour's shores.

As I neared, I could see that Morrison had moved to the yacht's stern, where he was attempting to disable my pursuit by firing shots at my boat's engine. The bullets sparked off the water around me, but the fog and the movement of both boats made accurate shooting nearly impossible.

I stayed as close as I dared while trying to anticipate where Hartwell would take the yacht. He needed deep water and privacy for what Morrison planned to do, but he also needed to avoid the shipping lanes where other vessels might witness the crime or careen into them.

The answer came to me as we passed under the Harbour Bridge—they were not headed for open water but likely the secluded coves near Middle Head, where the combination of deep water and rocky shores would provide perfect cover for the disposing of a body.

I cut across the harbour's main channel, taking a more direct route that would allow me to intercept the yacht before it reached its destination. The risk was enormous—if I miscalculated the timing or the yacht's course, Mrs Hartwell would die while I was racing through the fog toward empty water.

But luck was with me. As the yacht rounded the point near Middle Head, I was waiting in a small cove that blocked their escape route to their undoubted destination. Morrison was forced to slow the yacht and change course, giving me the opportunity I needed to close the distance between our boats.

I rammed the motorboat directly into the yacht's stern, sending them both stumbling as the larger vessel shuddered from the impact. The collision threw me forward, and I was able to leap aboard the yacht before they could recover his footing.

Morrison had another gun in his hand—Hartwell looked as though he was a deer caught in an automobile's headlights. Morrison's face was rent with a wild fury.

"Stay back, Collins!" he shouted, his voice cracking with hysteria. "I won't let you destroy the good thing we all have going."

Mrs Hartwell was tied to a chair in the yacht's main cabin, her eyes wide with terror as she watched this madman point a gun at the man trying to save her, with her husband apparently frozen with fear beside his erstwhile colleague-in-crime.

"It's over, Morrison," I said, moving carefully across the deck. "The police know about the smuggling operation, the lodge connection, everything. Surrender now and you might avoid the gallows."

"Never!" Morrison's hand shook as he tried to aim the gun. "The millions we're likely to make could balloon into even more in the years ahead. And, if Kozlov ever falls, I'm next in line to replace him."

He was mad with power and began firing wildly, the bullet splintering the yacht's cabin wall inches from my head. The recoil threw him off balance, and I lunged forward, grabbing for the weapon.

We struggled for control of the gun while the yacht rocked in the harbour swells. Morrison was strong, and I quickly wondered if he might overpower me. Obviously, Hartwell had thought along similar lines, and he joined the fray. Not against me, but against his now former colleague.

"Hartwell, what are you doing?" Morrison grunted.

"I won't let you kill my wife. She doesn't deserve any of this. I never wanted anyone to ever be hurt."

They struggled there, Hartwell, perhaps surprisingly, holding his own against his clearly stronger and more malicious enemy. All I could do was watch as they clawed and struggled together, wrestling for control of their destiny.

Suddenly, the gun skittered across the deck as Morrison broke free from Hartwell's grip. "Hartwell, you fool. I'll take care of you and your wife, I swear!"

"Never!"

And he lunged at the criminal, the two of them hurtling toward the rail, bashing against it. Morrison bore the brunt of it, crashing through it and plunging into the frigid waters of Sydney harbour. Hartwell was able to grab hold of a safety line and, as I moved forward to try and reach for him, his grip wavered, his feet slipped, and he, too, was instantly swallowed by the dark water below.

The splash echoed across the water, followed by a terrible silence that seemed to stretch on forever. Then, I thought I could hear the faint sound of police sirens, but they seemed impossibly far away, and I suddenly felt all alone in the darkness of the Sydney night.

~ Chapter 13 ~

I leaned over the yacht's rail, straining to see through the fog and darkness for any sign of movement in the black water below.

"Hartwell!" I called out, my voice carrying across the still harbour. "Are you there?"

There was no response except the gentle lapping of waves against the yacht's hull. The fog had thickened during the tail end of the struggle, reducing visibility to mere yards and muffling all sounds except the distant hum of the city.

I grabbed a life preserver from the yacht's emergency equipment and threw it toward the spot I thought Hartwell had disappeared, but the fog made it impossible to see where it landed. The harbour current was stronger than it appeared from the surface, and both Hartwell and Morrison could already be dozens of yards from the yacht, if not further.

"Help!" Mrs Hartwell's voice called from the cabin, where she remained tied to the chair. "Please, you have to save him!"

I found a flashlight in the yacht's equipment locker and began sweeping its beam across the water in expanding circles, searching for any sign of Hartwell's presence. The light barely penetrated the fog, creating ghostly reflections that could have been a man's head or simply the wake from a passing boat.

"Edgar never learned to swim!" Mrs Hartwell cried as I worked frantically to untie her bonds. "His father thought it was beneath a gentleman's dignity. Oh God, Edgar."

I freed her from the chair and helped her to the yacht's deck, where she immediately began calling her husband's name into the fog. Her voice was raw with desperation and guilt, the sound of a woman who realised she might be witnessing her husband's death despite all his crimes.

"We have to do something," she said, gripping my arm with surprising strength. "Whatever Edgar did, he doesn't deserve to drown like this."

I started the yacht's engines and began a systematic search pattern, using the boat's powerful spotlight to sweep the water while Mrs Hartwell continued calling Edgar's name. But the harbour was vast and dark, and the fog created a maze of false shadows and phantom reflections.

After twenty minutes of fruitless searching, I heard the sound of police boats approaching through the fog. Tom Majors had received my message through Pemberton, I fancied, and was coordinating a rescue operation, but I feared it was already too late.

The first police launch appeared through the fog like a ghost ship, its searchlight cutting through the darkness as it approached our position. Tom Majors stood on the bow, his face grim with the knowledge that we were probably searching for a body rather than a survivor.

"Magpie!" he called across the water. "What's the situation?"

"Edgar Hartwell went overboard during a struggle," I shouted back. "He can't swim, and he's been in the water for over twenty minutes."

"We'll coordinate a search pattern. You take the eastern sector while we cover the western approaches."

The search continued for another hour or so, with additional police boats and harbour patrol vessels joining the effort. The powerful searchlights turned the fog into a luminous maze, but they revealed nothing except empty water and the occasional piece of floating debris.

Mrs Hartwell stood at the yacht's rail throughout the search, her face pale and drawn as she watched the lights sweep back and forth across the harbour. She'd wrapped herself in a blanket from the cabin, but she continued to shiver despite the protection from the night air.

"I knew Edgar was involved in something illegal," she said quietly as we watched the search boats work. "The unexplained money, the nervous telephone calls, the way he avoided discussing his business activities. But I never imagined it involved murder."

"When did you first suspect?"

"Several months ago, when Charles Weatherby started visiting the house regularly. Edgar claimed it was business related to the import company, but Charles always seemed nervous and uncomfortable, like a man with something to hide."

"Why didn't you tell me all this earlier?"

"I didn't want to believe...I didn't really know for sure..."

It was the same old story. The wife suspected, then doubted her instincts, then came to believe in them again, but couldn't stand to do anything but embroil me in a pseudo-investigation mired in half-truths and innuendo. At least to start with.

I then thought about Charles's blackmail demands and the pressure they must have created in the Hartwell household. Hartwell had been living a double life, trying to maintain his respectable facade while dealing with increasingly dangerous criminal associates.

"Edgar mentioned that he believed Rose Murphy overheard one of his telephone conversations," Mrs Hartwell continued. "He was terrified that she would tell the police what she'd heard."

"Rose is safe," I assured her. "She's under police protection and will testify about what she overheard."

"Edgar never wanted to hurt anyone. I have to believe that. He was weak and frightened, but he wasn't naturally violent. It was that Morrison character who pushed him toward murder."

Which brought me back to the situation at hand. While Hartwell couldn't swim, and thus likely perished beneath the waves, Morrison was possibly another story entirely. The miscreant was strong, vital, and if he knew how to swim, it was very possible he was able to make his escape. I made a note to inform Tom of this at the earliest opportunity.

I gazed at Mrs Hartwell once more, and I realised that she was as much a victim of the conspiracy as Charles Weatherby had been. She'd been living with something of a stranger, unaware that her comfortable life was built on drug smuggling and corruption.

"Did you know about the stolen jewellery?" I asked.

She nodded slowly. "I suspected the theft was staged when Edgar seemed more relieved than upset about the insurance settlement. The pieces that were supposedly stolen were items I rarely wore, despite their sentimental value, almost as if someone had carefully selected them to minimize the personal financial loss."

"Hartwell needed the insurance money to pay Charles's blackmail demands. And when Charles demanded more than your husband could provide, he turned to Morrison for a permanent solution."

She sobbed at this and shivered in the chill of the night sea air. The knowledge of how completely she'd been deceived by the man she'd married—loved—must have cut deep.

The search boats continued their methodical pattern, but I could see from Tom's expression when his boat came near that hope was fading. The harbour waters were bitterly cold even in the relatively mild Sydney winter, and Hartwell had been submerged for nearly two hours now. Even if he'd managed to stay afloat initially, hypothermia would surely have claimed him by now.

It was Mrs Hartwell who spotted the body.

"There," she said quietly, pointing toward a section of water near the harbour's eastern shore. "Something's floating near those rocks."

One of the police launches immediately changed course toward the indicated area, its searchlight focusing on what appeared to be a dark shape bobbing among the rock formations. As the boat drew closer, the light revealed Edgar Hartwell's body, face down in the water and clearly beyond rescue.

The recovery operation was handled with professional efficiency, but I could see the impact on Mrs Hartwell as her husband's body was pulled from the harbour. Despite everything he had done, despite the crimes he'd committed and the people he'd betrayed, she was watching the death of the man she still loved.

"He was a good man once," she said, tears streaming down her face, as we watched the police launch carry Hartwell body toward the marina. "Before the greed and the fear corrupted everything he touched."

We then made our way back to Rose Bay, and Mrs Hartwell began to reveal more details about her husband's activities—what little she knew of the conspiracy that had ultimately destroyed him. Her information amongst everything else I had uncovered would be crucial for completing the investigation and bringing the remaining conspirators to justice.

"Edgar kept a safe deposit box at the Bank of New South Wales," she said. "He thought I didn't know about it, but I'd seen the key among his personal effects. He mentioned once that it contained 'insurance' for difficult times."

"The stolen jewellery?"

"I assume so. Edgar was paranoid about being betrayed, has been the entire time I've known him. I don't know if that means anything to you, but..."

This was an interesting development. Perhaps Hartwell kept certain records in that safe, as well as the missing jewellery. If that was the case, it would provide the finishing touch to the entire case, the perfect ammunition necessary to bring down the entire network.

"There's something else," Mrs Hartwell continued. "Edgar and Pemberton were particularly close. I think he may have been involved in everything."

The revelation that Pemberton was also part of the conspiracy explained how the fake jewellery theft had been orchestrated with such precision. The butler had provided detailed information about the house's layout, the location of the safe, and the timing of the charity gala.

"Pemberton knew about the combination to the safe?"

"He shouldn't have, under normal circumstances, but I'm fairly certain he did. Just the things he'd said, the way he sometimes behaved."

As we reached the Rose Bay marina, I could see Tom had beaten us there. He was waiting on the dock with his team of detectives and medical personnel. With Edgar Hartwell now dead, the focus of the investigation would shift to dismantling the remaining conspiracy. And arresting everyone involved. But time was of the essence.

"Mrs Hartwell," Tom said gently as we disembarked from the yacht, "I'm sorry for your loss, but I need to ask you some questions about your husband's activities and associates."

"I understand, chief. I want to help in any way I can to see justice done for Charles Weatherby and to expose the corruption that destroyed my marriage."

As the police began processing the scene and taking Mrs Hartwell's statement, I reflected on the tragic ending to Edgar Hartwell's life. He'd been a weak man who'd allowed greed and fear to corrupt his judgment, but he'd also been trapped by circumstances that had spiraled beyond his control.

The smuggling operation had begun as a relatively minor tax avoidance scheme but had evolved into a major drug trafficking network that required violence to maintain. Hartwell had lacked the criminal experience to navigate such dangerous waters, and his association with professional killers like Morrison and the true mastermind of the operation, Kozlov, had ultimately cost him everything.

But his death didn't end the conspiracy—it simply removed one participant from a network that included corrupt officials, medical professionals, and organised criminals who would continue their operations unless stopped by aggressive police action.

The key to dismantling the network lay in the possible evidence Hartwell had kept in his safe deposit box. If there was such evidence there—and I thought it highly likely—then that, on top of the other evidence I'd accumulated, and the testimony of witnesses like Mrs Hartwell and Rose Murphy, would put the case beyond all doubt. With Hartwell dead, the remaining conspirators would be scrambling to protect themselves and eliminate any evidence that could link them to the crimes. We had to move fast.

Dr Malcolm Sinclair would undoubtedly be trying to destroy any medical records that connected him to Charles's murder. Dennis Fletcher would be attempting to eliminate customs documents that showed his corruption. Robert Manning would be working to cover up his role in facilitating the dock operations.

And Viktor Kozlov would be planning to eliminate anyone who could testify about the Harbour Club's role in coordinating the criminal network.

The web of corruption was beginning to unravel, but the predators caught in that web would fight back with increasing desperation as they realised their entire criminal empire was threatened. The next few days would determine whether justice would prevail or whether the conspiracy would succeed in covering up its crimes through violence and intimidation.

As Mrs Hartwell was escorted to the police station to give her formal statement, I realised she represented both the human cost of the conspiracy and the hope for its ultimate exposure. Her courage in revealing what she knew of her husband's crimes—little enough as it may have been—would nevertheless be crucial for ensuring that Charles Weatherby's murder didn't go unpunished and that the corruption poisoning Sydney's institutions was finally brought to light.

~ Chapter 14 ~

Dawn was breaking over Sydney as Tom and the rest of the city's police division coordinated the raids that would bring down the remaining conspirators. Thankfully, due to my indepth involvement in the entire case, Tom had allowed me to tag along. Edgar Hartwell's death had removed an important figure in the smuggling operation, but the network of corruption he'd been a small part of remained dangerous and determined to protect itself.

The first target was the Pyrmont warehouse where I'd witnessed the opium processing operation. While I had witnessed the partial removal of much of the evidence, there was still enough left over to add to the burgeoning pile of evidence we had been compiling. A team of police constables surrounded the building while Tom and I approached the main entrance with warrants for search and arrest. There were no drugs remaining on site, but there were plenty of Chinese workers left, moving about equipment and other paraphernalia. All were taken without issue.

Next up was the warehouse in Woolloomooloo that I had overheard Morrison talking about, its location obtained from one of the less brave Chinese workers left to take the fall back in Pyrmont. The operation proceeded smoothly and with the kind of efficiency that came from knowing you were about to ensnare one of the most dangerous criminal gangs in all of Sydney.

The warehouse was bustling with activity despite the early hour. Jimmy Morrison—he had clearly made it to safety after his dunk in Sydney Harbour—was directing a crew of workers who were frantically loading crates onto trucks, clearly attempting to move the operation before the police could intervene. He was too late.

"Police! Nobody move!" Tom shouted as we burst through the warehouse doors.

Morrison's hand went immediately to his jacket, but he found himself facing a dozen armed constables who'd positioned themselves throughout the building. The workers scattered in panic, but there was nowhere to run in the enclosed space.

"Jimmy Morrison," Tom announced formally, "you're under arrest for the murder of Charles Weatherby and conspiracy to smuggle illegal narcotics."

Morrison's face showed no emotion as the handcuffs were applied. He was a professional criminal who understood that arrest was always a possibility in his line of work. But I could see calculation in his eyes as he evaluated his options for avoiding the gallows. I doubted there were any.

The warehouse yielded a treasure trove of evidence. Hundreds of pounds of raw opium were found hidden in tea crates, along with processing equipment and distribution records that detailed the scope of the operation. More importantly, we discovered paperwork which contained names, dates, and payment records for much of the operation.

While some trusted officers remained behind to process the warehouse evidence, Tom, several more officers and I moved on to our next target—Dr Malcolm Sinclair's medical practice near Macquarie Street. The doctor's involvement in Charles's murder made him one of the most dangerous conspirators, and his medical knowledge gave him the skills to destroy evidence effectively.

We found Dr Sinclair in his office, burning documents in the fireplace. His usually immaculate appearance was disheveled, and his hands shook as he fed papers to the flames.

"Dr Sinclair," Tom said, showing his warrant, "you're under arrest for the murder of Charles Weatherby."

The doctor's composure cracked completely. "I never wanted anyone to die," he said, his voice barely above a whisper. "Edgar asked me to provide medical consultation for a business associate who was having drug problems." It was a blatant lie.

"You injected Charles Weatherby with a fatal dose of morphine," I said coldly.

"Edgar said it was to help Charles overcome his addiction! I thought I was providing medical treatment, not committing murder!"

The lie was pathetic, and Dr Sinclair knew it. His medical expertise made it impossible to claim ignorance about the effects of the massive morphine dose he'd administered. But desperation was making him grasp at any story that might save him from the gallows.

The search of Sinclair's office revealed additional evidence of the conspiracy. Hidden behind medical texts, we found detailed notes about morphine dosages and injection techniques that had clearly been used to plan not only Charles's murder, but others over a number of years. Sinclair was, in effect, a mass murderer for hire. There were also records of payments from Edgar Hartwell, disguised as fees for treating "industrial accidents" among dock workers.

Our third target was Dennis Fletcher, the corrupt customs inspector whose position had made the smuggling operation possible. We found him at his office in Customs House, frantically shredding documents while his secretary looked on in utter bewilderment.

Fletcher was a small, nervous man who'd clearly been living beyond his means. His office was furnished with expensive items that his government salary couldn't possibly afford, and his desperation was evident in every movement as he tried to destroy incriminating evidence.

"Mr Fletcher," Tom announced, "you're under arrest for conspiracy to smuggle illegal narcotics and corruption of public office."

"I never knew what was in those shipments," Fletcher protested as the handcuffs were applied. "Edgar Hartwell told me they were luxury goods to avoid excessive taxation. I thought I was just helping a legitimate businessman reduce his operating costs."

Another pathetic lie. The documents Fletcher had been trying to destroy told a different story. Shipping manifests with deliberate omissions, inspection schedules that had been manipulated to avoid detection, and records of substantial payments from Hartwell's company painted a clear picture of systematic corruption. We had arrived in time to obtain much of what he wouldn't have wanted us to see.

Robert Manning, the dock supervisor, proved more elusive. When we arrived at the dock offices, we found that Manning had failed to report for work and his home address led us to an empty house with signs of hasty departure. He'd apparently fled Sydney during the night, possibly warned by associates who'd observed our other arrests.

But Manning's flight only delayed the inevitable. The evidence we'd gathered from the warehouse and customs office included detailed records of his involvement in the smuggling operation. Warrants were issued for his arrest, and his description was circulated to police forces throughout Australia.

The most challenging target was the malicious spider at the heart of this web of crime and corruption—Viktor Kozlov and the Harbour Club operation. The gambling establishment was hidden beneath Romano's Restaurant, and Kozlov's network of criminal associates made a direct assault extremely dangerous.

Tom had assembled a large team of experienced constables for the raid, including several officers who'd dealt with organised crime in the past. We approached the restaurant during the lunch hour, when legitimate diners would provide cover for our operation.

Giuseppe, the maître d', tried to deny knowledge of any basement gambling operation, but a warrant allowed us to search the entire building. The basement stairs were locked and barricaded, suggesting that Kozlov had been preparing for a police raid.

When we finally gained access to the basement, we found the Harbour Club in the process of being dismantled. Gaming equipment was being loaded into crates while Kozlov's men worked frantically to remove any evidence of illegal activities.

Kozlov himself was nowhere to be found. His security chief informed us that the Russian had left Sydney on an overnight ship to Hong Kong, taking with him the club's financial records and client lists that would have provided crucial evidence about the conspiracy's reach into Sydney society. The loss of the true leader of the entire criminal operation infuriated me, but perhaps his capture had been a forlorn hope from the outset. In my experience, the highest rung in the criminal ladder often evaded final justice, frustrating as that always was.

But we did arrest several of Kozlov's associates, along with corrupt police officers and government officials who'd been meeting at the club to coordinate their criminal activities. The basement yielded evidence of systematic bribery and corruption that reached into the highest levels of Sydney's establishment.

And, as expected, we recovered the stolen jewellery from Mrs Hartwell's collection in Hartwell's safe deposit box, along with the added bonanza of information that he had collected linking everyone in the organisation together—their names, roles and more. As I'd hoped, this was the final piece that tied everything together, and what would ultimately put everyone involved away for a very long time.

As the day progressed and the arrests mounted, I reflected on the scope of corruption we'd uncovered. The smuggling operation had been far more than a simple criminal enterprise—it had been a cancer that had infected Sydney's most trusted institutions.

The masonic lodge that Edgar Hartwell had used to recruit conspirators would face a scandal that would destroy its reputation and force the examination of similar organizations throughout Australia. The customs service would require a comprehensive investigation to identify other corrupt officials. The medical profession would be forced to confront the reality that one of their own had used his knowledge to commit mass murder.

But it was the human cost that affected me most deeply. Charles Weatherby—hardly an innocent, it had to be said—had died because he'd threatened to expose the corruption, but his death had also been the consequence of a gambling addiction that had made him vulnerable to criminal exploitation and to attempting his own, nefarious way—blackmail—of escaping his troubles.

Mrs Hartwell had lost her husband and her comfortable life, but she'd gained something more valuable—the knowledge that she'd helped bring his killers to justice. Her cooperation with the investigation had been crucial for understanding the full scope of the conspiracy.

Rose Murphy had risked her life to testify about what she'd overheard, demonstrating a courage that far exceeded what should be expected from someone in her position. Her willingness to speak truth to power had helped expose the corruption that had claimed Charles's life. I made a promise to myself—as well as to her—that I would do all I can to help her secure a new position after all this was done.

As evening approached, Tom and I returned to Phillip Street to review the evidence we'd gathered and discuss the next phase of the operation—the prosecution of the arrested conspirators. The cases would be complex, involving multiple jurisdictions and requiring testimony from witnesses who might face retaliation from criminal associates still at large.

"This is the biggest corruption case Sydney has ever seen," Tom said as we examined the documents recovered from the various raids. "The newspapers are going to have a field day with the masonic lodge connection and the involvement of supposedly respectable professionals."

"We have enough on all of them to convict," I said.

"Morrison and Sinclair are facing murder charges based on irrefutable evidence. They'll both be facing a death sentence. Fletcher's corruption is documented in his own records. With everything else we have, I don't see any of the others getting off without many years hard labour."

The paperwork we had found at the Harbour Club, with its detailed records of payments and activities, the concise details in Edgar Hartwell's safe, my own accumulated evidence, combined with Mrs Hartwell's testimony about her husband's confessions and Rose Murphy's account of the telephone conversation she'd overheard, we had an ironclad case against the surviving conspirators.

But I also knew that powerful forces would work to minimize the scandal and protect the reputations of the institutions that had been corrupted. The masonic lodge would claim that Edgar Hartwell had acted independently, betraying his oath rather than representing systemic problems. The medical association would argue that Dr Sinclair was an aberration rather than an example of professional corruption. I was well aware of all that.

"What about the missing conspirators?" I asked. "Manning is still free and the mastermind behind it all, Kozlov, has fled the country."

"We'll find Manning eventually," Tom said with assuredness. "Men like him can't disappear completely, and his criminal record will make it difficult for him to find legitimate employment. As for Kozlov, we can escalate our investigation to the international level, but if he's returned to Russia, I have grave fears he'll never face justice for his crimes."

That was a hard truth to swallow, but not an unexpected one. I had to make do with the knowledge we had destroyed an entire criminal organisation intent on murder and misery. That would have to be enough.

As Tom completed his paperwork and prepared to release information to the press, I realised that the case had changed me as much as it had exposed the corruption in Sydney society. My background as a former criminal had provided unique insights into the investigation, but it had also reminded me of how easily people could cross the line between right and wrong.

The web of corruption that had been uncovered had been built by men who'd started with small compromises—avoiding taxes, accepting modest bribes, looking the other way when suspicious activities occurred. But each compromise had led to larger ones, until they'd become trapped in a criminal conspiracy that required murder to maintain.

The reckoning was far from complete. The trials would take months, and some of those involved—Morrison in particular—would likely play dirty as much as they could. I, however, had confidence that the strength of the evidence obtained would not allow any dodging of justice. Most importantly, the people of Sydney could feel safer knowing that the criminals who'd been poisoning their community with illegal drugs had finally been brought to justice.

Charles Weatherby's murder had been avenged, but more importantly, his death had led to the exposure of corruption that might have continued for years if left unchecked. In the end, perhaps that was the best memorial a young man could have—knowing that his death had served the cause of justice and protected others from similar fates.

~ Chapter 15 ~

The morning sun streamed through the windows of my Castlereagh Street office as I sat at my desk, writing the final report on the Hartwell case for my own records. Three weeks had passed since Edgar Hartwell's body was pulled from Sydney Harbour, and the ripple effects of the investigation continued to spread through the city's establishment like cracks in a foundation.

My fountain pen scratched across the paper as I documented the last details of the conspiracy that had claimed Charles Weatherby's life and exposed corruption reaching into Sydney's most trusted institutions. The final tally was impressive in its scope. Jimmy Morrison had been sentenced to hang for Charles's murder, his professional demeanor surprisingly cracking completely when the judge pronounced the death sentence. Dr Malcolm Sinclair, in something of a twist, escaped the death penalty and received twenty years for his role in the killing instead. While his medical career was destroyed along with his freedom, his stellar reputation within the medical community was, apparently, what had saved his life. Dennis Fletcher got fifteen years for corruption, his comfortable government pension replaced by a prison cell.

Robert Manning had been captured attempting to board a cargo ship in Melbourne, his flight having lasted only two weeks before dock workers recognised his description. Viktor Kozlov's final destination remained unclear, but it was assumed he had indeed returned to mother Russia, his freedom and no doubt some of his ill-begotten wealth, intact. Whether he could stake a position there to the same lofty extent he had achieved here in Sydney, Australia, would likely forever remain a mystery.

The masonic lodge connection had created the biggest scandal, with newspaper headlines screaming about 'Secret Society Corruption' and 'Brotherhood of Thieves.' The lodge itself would undoubtedly survive, but several prominent members had quietly resigned, and the organisation would likely face years of scrutiny from authorities and the public.

A soft knock interrupted my writing. Mrs Evelyn Hartwell entered, dressed in black but carrying herself with a poise that hadn't been present during our first meeting. The frightened woman who'd hired me to investigate a jewellery theft had been replaced by someone who'd found strength in the truth, however painful it might be.

"Mr Collins," she said, settling into the chair across from my desk. "I wanted to thank you one final time before I leave Sydney."

"Leaving? Where are you headed?"

"Melbourne, as soon as possible, in fact. I have a sister there, and the scandal has made it almost impossible to remain here. Every time I walk down the street, I can feel people staring and whispering about Edgar's crimes." She paused, smoothing her black dress. "But I'm grateful you helped expose the truth. Charles Weatherby deserved justice, and his family deserved to know who killed their son. And, as much as I still loved my husband, I deserve to be free from such a horrendous position amongst such evil."

I set down my pen and studied her face. The past month had aged her, but there was peace there too—the kind that comes from no longer living with secrets and lies.

"Have you decided what to do with the insurance settlement?"

"I'm donating it all to the Children's Hospital, as I mentioned. Dr Sinclair organised that charity gala to provide cover for the robbery, so it seems fitting that some good should come from Edgar's crimes." She reached into her purse and withdrew an envelope. "This is for you—the final payment for your services, plus a bonus for the dangers you faced...and for saving my life."

I opened the envelope and found more money than we'd agreed upon. "This is too much, Mrs Hartwell."

"As I said, some good has come from all this, and those that deserve reward have, I feel, received such. Including you. For my life, and my honour, I thank you." She stood to leave, then paused. "May I ask you something personal?"

"Of course."

"How does someone like you—someone with your background—develop such a strong sense of justice?"

It was a good question, but not a hard one to answer. "Maybe because I know what it's like to be on the wrong side of the law. I understand how easy it is to compromise your principles for money or convenience. But I also learned that there's more satisfaction in helping people than in taking advantage of them. And I don't like bullies."

She nodded thoughtfully. "Edgar never learned that lesson. He had everything a man could want—wealth, social position, a comfortable life—but it wasn't enough. He always wanted more, and that greed destroyed him."

After she left, I returned to my report, but my thoughts kept drifting to the personal cost of the investigation. The case had forced me to confront my own past in ways I hadn't expected, or particularly wanted, particularly my relationship with Mary.

She had played a small but also crucial role in the investigation, providing information about Charles Weatherby's attempts to sell "family heirlooms" and later helping me understand the criminal networks involved in the conspiracy. But our reunion had stirred up emotions I'd tried to bury since leaving my criminal life behind.

The night I'd spent with Mary while visiting her antique shop had reminded me of what we'd once shared—the excitement of dangerous enterprises, the intimacy of shared secrets, and the peculiar trust that exists between partners in crime. But it had also highlighted the gulf that now separated us.

Mary remained on the borderland between legitimate and criminal activity, running her antique shop as a front for occasional fencing operations and maintaining contacts in Sydney's underworld. She claimed to be 'mostly honest' these days, but I knew she'd cross the line again if the right opportunity presented itself.

I cared for her—perhaps even loved her still—but I couldn't build a future with someone who refused to fully embrace the law-abiding life I'd chosen. The work I was doing as a private investigator had given me a sense of purpose I'd never found as a jewel thief, and I couldn't risk that redemption for even the deepest personal connection. While there was still a strong connection between us, it would forever remain fleeting. Because it had to be.

The telephone rang, interrupting my brooding. It was Tom with news about the ongoing investigations spawned by the Hartwell case.

"Magpie, good to find you in. Thought you'd like to know that Fletcher's cooperation has led to three more arrests in the customs service. The corruption was more widespread than we initially thought."

"Doesn't surprise me," I replied. "Such an organisation had to run deep. Anything else you want to tell me?"

"Two more masonic lodges are under investigation, but nothing as extensive as Hartwell's operation. Most of the members seem to have been unaware of the criminal activities." Tom paused. "There's something else. Something much more unexpected. We've received word from Hong Kong that Kozlov was found dead in his hotel room there yesterday—apparently poisoned."

Hong Kong? Had he been making a potential journey back to that area? Or had he never actually reached Russia as we had guessed? Or was his presence in Hong Kong related to his drug smuggling operations? If so, then perhaps his fate wasn't entirely surprising. If the Chinese tongs had held Kozlov responsible for the loss of the entire nationwide operation in Australia, then even someone like him would not be able to evade their vengeance for long.

"That really does put an end to this case," Tom said with a hint of triumph.

After Tom hung up, I walked to my office window and looked out at the bustling street below. Castlereagh Street was full of people going about their daily business—clerks hurrying to appointments, shoppers examining window displays, businessmen discussing deals over lunch.

Most of them were honest citizens trying to make an honest living, but my investigation had reminded me how thin the line could be between respectability and corruption. I'd been fortunate in my life to find a path back to respectability, with the help of Tom Majors, and through my work as a private investigator. The skills I'd developed as a thief—reading people's motivations, understanding criminal networks, thinking like someone who operates outside the law—had proven valuable for legitimate purposes.

But redemption was an ongoing process, not a single decision. Every case offered the temptation to take shortcuts, to bend the rules for expediency or profit. The difference between my old life and my new one wasn't the absence of opportunity for wrongdoing—it was the choice to resist those opportunities.

My thoughts ultimately came to rest upon Viktor Kozlov. The mastermind behind the entire criminal operation, he had first escaped capture only to confront the ultimate judgement. He had perished, most likely at the hands of his 'Chinese partners.' The irony of it all was not lost on me.

A knock at the door interrupted my philosophical reflections. A middle-aged woman entered, clutching a small handbag and looking around nervously at my modest office furnishings.

"Mr Collins? I'm Mrs Elizabeth Hanson. I need help finding my missing daughter."

I gestured for her to take a seat, already feeling the familiar stirring of professional interest. Another case, another opportunity to use my unusual background in service of justice rather than just personal gain.

"Tell me about your daughter, Mrs Hanson."

As she began describing her missing child and the circumstances of her disappearance, I reflected on the satisfaction I'd found in my new profession. The work was dangerous and often poorly paid, but it provided something I'd never experienced as a criminal—the knowledge that my efforts were helping people rather than exploiting them.

The Hartwell case had been complex and challenging, involving murder, corruption, and criminal networks that reached into Sydney's highest social circles. But it had also demonstrated that justice was possible, even when the perpetrators held positions of trust and respectability.

Charles Weatherby's murder had been avenged, and the corruption that enabled it had been exposed and punished. Mrs Hartwell had found the courage to rebuild her life on a foundation of truth rather than comfortable lies. Rose Murphy had discovered that ordinary people could stand up to powerful criminals and make a difference.

And I had learned that redemption wasn't just possible—it was an ongoing choice that had to be made every day, with every case, in every decision to serve justice rather than personal interest.

My criminal past would always be part of who I was, but it no longer defined my future. The skills I'd learned as a thief could be used to catch other thieves. The understanding I'd gained of criminal psychology could help protect innocent victims. The network of contacts I'd developed in Sydney's underworld could serve the cause of law and order.

As Mrs Hanson finished describing her missing daughter, I reached for a fresh notepad and began taking detailed notes. Another case was beginning, another opportunity to prove that people could change, that past mistakes didn't have to determine future actions.

The weak winter sunlight streaming through my office window seemed brighter as I began planning the investigation that would help a mother find her lost child. Outside, Sydney continued its busy life, unaware that in a modest second-floor office on Castlereagh Street, a former criminal was writing another chapter in his unlikely journey toward redemption.

The Magpie had found his true calling at last—not in taking from others, but often in helping them recover what had been lost.

~ Acknowledgements ~

An abundance of thank-yous to my Glowing Eyes Media team—Chaz and Claude, as well as to my family for always supporting me and being by my side every step of the way. Thank you also to everyone who has taken this series, and this character, into their hearts—you the readers. I forever remain in your gratitude. I hope you also enjoyed this one. I feel like I'm really getting into my stride with this series, with this style of writing, now. A preview of the next in the series, *The Lost Boy*, follows.

I promise many more George 'Magpie' Collins mysteries to come.

Take care.

Frank Dirscherl aka Len Driscoll
Wollongong, 2025

THE LOST BOY

~ Sneak peek ~

Here is a special sneak peek at the following novel in the series, *The Lost Boy.* Please enjoy chapter 1 of this exciting book...

~ Chapter 1 ~

The warm late spring afternoon hung over Hyde Park like a promise of the summer to come. November in Sydney could be unpredictable—one day you'd be reaching for your coat, the next you'd be loosening your tie and looking for shade. This Friday was one of the good ones, the kind that made you forget there was work waiting back at the office.

I'd claimed a bench with a decent view of the Archibald Fountain and settled in to watch the world go by. People-watching was more than just a pleasant way to pass time in my line of work—it was professional development. You learned to read the signs, to spot the tells that separated the honest citizens from the ones who bore watching. The way a man's eyes moved when he thought no one was looking. The way a woman clutched her handbag when she walked past certain types. The small movements and gestures that spoke louder than words ever could.

The park was busy but not crowded. Office workers were making the most of their lunch breaks, jackets slung over arms, ties loosened against the warming air. A group of young mothers had spread blankets near the Domain Road entrance, their children playing some elaborate game that seemed to involve a great deal of running and shouting. An elderly gentleman in a panama hat was feeding the birds with methodical precision, doling out breadcrumbs like a banker counting notes.

I'd been there maybe twenty minutes when she caught my attention.

She was sitting on a bench perhaps thirty yards from mine, under a copse of oversized fig trees. Quality, you could see it from here. The sort of woman who'd never set foot in a pub but could probably tell you the vintage of any wine you cared to name. Mid-twenties, I'd guess, with dark hair pinned up under a small hat that probably cost more than most men made in a month. Her dress was navy blue, well-cut, expensive. The kind of outfit you wore when you had somewhere important to be, or when you wanted people to know you had the money for somewhere important to be.

The boy with her was maybe five years old, dressed in a blue sailor suit that looked like it had been pressed that morning. Everything about him spoke of care and money—from his polished shoes to the way his dark hair had been combed and oiled into perfect order. He had that restless energy that boys his age carried like a disease, constantly moving even when he was trying to sit still.

His mother—had to be his mother from the way she watched him—had brought a book, something thick and serious-looking. But she wasn't really reading. Her eyes kept moving from the page to the boy and back again, the way mothers did when they were trying to relax but couldn't quite manage it.

The boy was more interested in the pigeons that strutted about the park looking for scraps. He'd slide off the bench, take a few steps toward them, and his mother would call him back without looking up from her book. It was a dance they'd probably performed a hundred times before.

I was thinking about heading back to Castlereagh Street— the Anderson insurance case wouldn't solve itself—when the black Essex sedan caught my eye.

It was idling at the kerb near College Street, exhaust wisping in the warm air. Nothing unusual about that, except for the way it sat there. Patient. Watchful. The engine was running but nobody got out, nobody got in. Just sitting there like it was waiting for something.

The car was maybe three years old, well-maintained but not flashy. Black paint job, probably factory original. Clean enough to be respectable, dirty enough not to stand out. The sort of vehicle that would disappear in traffic, which was exactly what you'd want if you were doing something you didn't want remembered.

I couldn't make out the occupants clearly through the windscreen. Two shapes, maybe three. The driver was wearing what looked like a dark hat, pulled low. Professional criminals, in my experience, understood the value of looking ordinary.

Something about the Essex bothered me. Maybe it was the way it was positioned—angled so the driver had a clear view of the park, specifically the area where the woman and boy were sitting. Maybe it was just the old thief's instincts, the ones that had kept me out of gaol back when I was working the other side of the law. Either way, I found myself watching the car instead of the people.

The boy had convinced his mother to let him feed the pigeons. She'd given him what looked like the remains of a sandwich, warning him about something—probably not to get his shoes dirty or fall in the water. He'd trotted off toward the fountain with the casual confidence of childhood, scattering crumbs to an eager crowd of pigeons and sparrows.

His mother watched him go, then returned to her book. But I noticed she kept glancing up, checking on him every few seconds. The maternal radar that never quite switched off.

That's when the Essex moved.

Not fast, not drawing attention. Just a smooth pull away from the kerb and a casual turn into the park entrance. The kind of movement you'd make if you belonged there, if you had every right to be driving through Hyde Park on a warm Friday afternoon.

But I was watching, and I saw the way the car positioned itself. Saw the way it rolled to a stop about twenty feet from where the boy was feeding the ducks. Saw the doors open with the synchronised precision of a rehearsed operation.

Two men got out. One tall and thin, one shorter and stockier. Both wearing dark suits, both moving with the kind of deliberate calm that spoke of planning and practice. They weren't running, weren't shouting, weren't doing anything that would attract attention from casual observers.

They were just two men walking purposefully toward a five-year-old boy who was completely absorbed in watching the birds squabble over his breadcrumbs.

I was moving before my brain had fully processed what I was seeing. Something was wrong—badly wrong—and every instinct I'd developed in over thirty-five years of living was screaming at me to do something about it.

The tall man reached the boy first. One moment the child was laughing at a particularly aggressive pigeon, the next he was being scooped up in arms that knew exactly what they were doing. The boy's startled cry cut through the afternoon air like a knife through silk.

I was running now, my feet pounding across the grass, but thirty yards might as well have been thirty miles. The shorter man was already at the car, yanking open the rear door. The tall man bundled the boy inside, all flailing legs and sailor suit, while the child's cries grew higher and more desperate.

Behind me, I heard the woman scream. A sound that would probably wake me up for months to come.

The car doors slammed shut with the finality of a coffin lid. The driver—I caught a glimpse of him now, another dark shape under a pulled-down hat—threw the Essex into gear. Gravel sprayed from the rear wheels as the sedan lurched forward, taking the curve toward the park exit faster than safety recommended.

I kept running, chasing the black shape as it headed for College Street. My lungs were burning and my heart was hammering against my ribs, but I pushed harder, trying to close the gap. Trying to do something, anything, to stop what was happening.

By the time I reached the park gates, the Essex had disappeared into the afternoon traffic. I stood there gasping, scanning the stream of cars, trams, and horse-drawn carts that made up Sydney's daily chaos. Nothing. Just the usual collection of vehicles going about their lawful business.

The boy was gone.

I walked back toward the fountain, my mind already working despite the shock. In my former profession, as well as my years as an investigator, you learned to notice details even when everything was going to hell. Especially then. The difference between freedom and a stretch in Long Bay often came down to remembering the right detail at the right time.

The Essex had been a 1932 or '33 model, I was reasonably sure. Black paint, factory job rather than a respray. The number plate had been partially obscured—deliberately, I'd bet money on it—but I'd caught fragments. Numbers: 4 and 7, possibly an 8. NSW plates, which didn't narrow things down much in a city the size of Sydney.

The tall man had been the key player, the one who'd actually grabbed the boy. Dark suit, probably navy blue. White shirt, dark tie. Nothing distinctive about the clothing, which was almost certainly the point. But I'd seen something else as he'd lifted the child—a scar across the back of his right hand, running diagonally from his wrist toward his knuckles. Old and white, the kind you get from a blade rather than an accident.

The shorter man I'd seen less clearly, but he'd moved like muscle. Thick through the shoulders, heavy hands. The kind of man you hired when you needed something physical done and didn't want to do it yourself.

The driver had been just a shadow under his hat, but he'd known what he was doing. The way he'd positioned the car, the smooth acceleration, the timing—all of it spoke of practice and planning.

This hadn't been opportunistic. Someone had been watching, waiting, choosing their moment. They'd wanted this specific boy, not just any convenient target.

I could hear voices behind me, people starting to gather around the woman. Someone would call for the police soon, and then this place would be crawling with constables asking questions and taking measurements. All the proper procedures that usually accomplished bugger all when children's lives were at stake.

But I had something the police wouldn't have, at least not right away. I had a description of the car, partial plates, and most importantly, I had the scar. In my experience, scars were better than photographs when it came to identifying criminals. You could change your hair, grow a beard, put on weight or take it off. But scars were permanent, and this one was distinctive enough to pick out of a crowd.

The woman's sobs were carrying across the park now, the sound of a mother's heart breaking in real time. Other people were starting to converge on the scene—office workers abandoning their lunches, mothers gathering their own children closer, an elderly man who'd been reading his newspaper now standing and looking around in confusion.

I stayed on the edge of the growing crowd, listening but not interfering. Not yet. There would be time for questions later, when the immediate shock had worn off and people could think clearly again. Right now, the most important thing was to lock in what I'd seen while it was still fresh.

The Essex sedan, black, 1932 or '33 model. Partial plate: 4, 7, maybe 8. Three men: tall thin one with the diagonal scar on his right hand, shorter stocky one built like muscle, driver in a dark hat who knew his business. Professional job, planned and executed with military precision.

And somewhere in Sydney, a five-year-old boy in a sailor suit was probably crying for his mother.

I lit a cigarette and took a long drag, letting the tobacco settle my nerves. In my line of work, you saw plenty of ugly things. Husbands who beat their wives, wives who poisoned their husbands, business partners who'd sell their mothers for a percentage point. But there was something about crimes against children that got under your skin and stayed there.

Maybe it was because children were genuinely innocent, or maybe it was because they were helpless in a way that adults never quite were. Either way, watching that boy get bundled into the Essex had triggered something in me that went deeper than professional interest.

The crowd around the woman was growing. Someone had gone to find a constable, and I could see people looking around, probably wondering what to do next. Soon there would be questions, statements, the whole machinery of official investigation that would eventually grind into motion.

But official investigations took time, and time was something that kidnapped children didn't have much of. The first few hours were crucial. Every minute that passed made the trail colder, the chances of a good outcome smaller.

I finished my cigarette and ground the butt under my heel. The afternoon was still warm, still beautiful, but something had changed. The innocence had gone out of it, the way it always did when evil showed its face in broad daylight.

I found myself thinking about the scar on the tall man's hand. Distinctive marks like that didn't just disappear. Someone, somewhere, would remember seeing it. In a pub, maybe, or a boarding house, or one of the dozen places where Sydney's criminal element gathered to drink and plan their next job.

~ Also Available ~

A George 'Magpie' Collins Mystery #1

THE BROKEN CHAIN

Len Driscoll

In depression-era Sydney, young Charlie Bristow has vanished without a trace. Enter George 'Magpie' Collins, ex-con turned private investigator, hired to find the troubled youth As he delves into the shadows of the city, Collins must navigate the murky waters of deception and bring justice to a broken chain.

NOW AVAILABLE!

www.glowingeyesmedia.com

A George 'Magpie' Collins Mystery #2
THE BLACK SEAM
Len Driscoll

When psychiatrist Eleanor Whitman receives a chilling blackmail threat, she turns to George 'Magpie' Collins for help. But what begins as a case of quiet extortion quickly leads the detective deep into a web of medical manipulation, corporate corruption, and a deadly mining disaster long buried beneath the coalfields of Wollongong.

NOW AVAILABLE!

www.glowingeyesmedia.com

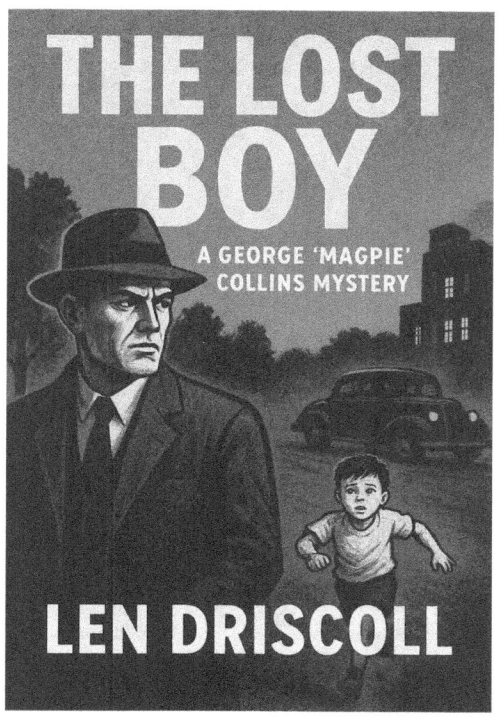

A George 'Magpie' Collins Mystery #4

THE LOST BOY

Len Driscoll

Sydney 1935. A late spring afternoon in Hyde Park shatters when a young boy is taken in broad daylight. Witnessing the abduction, George 'Magpie' Collins is drawn into a case that cuts to the heart of power, money and betrayal To save the boy, Collins must untangle a web of lies where family loyalty and criminal greed collide, and where one wrong move could mean another life lost.

COMING SOON!

www.glowingeyesmedia.com

The Wraith Dread Avenger of the Underworld #1
THE WRAITH
Frank Dirscherl

In a world not far removed from our own, a city lies ravaged. Crime overruns its streets, its citizens are helpless. Crime lord Robert Latham holds the city in his sway. One man, however, stands above the rest, willing to fight for freedom. That man is The Wraith!

NOW AVAILABLE!

www.glowingeyesmedia.com

The Wraith Dread Avenger of the Underworld #2
VALLEY OF EVIL
Frank Dirscherl

After the horror the Cobra unleashed upon Metro City, Paul Sanderson has recuperated, regained his strength and focus, and the city has been rebuilt while its citizens have slowly started to regroup and move forward. Into this relative calm marches Ma Tzi, the Hong Kong drug lord, who senses a weakness in resident crime lord Robert Latham's hold on the city and intends to exploit that in any way necessary. And at any cost.

NOW AVAILABLE!

www.glowingeyesmedia.com

The Wraith Dread Avenger of the Underworld #3
CROSSFIRE
Frank Dirscherl & Stephen J. Semones

After a terrorist attack leaves the citizens of Metro City reeling, an enigmatic stranger emerges from the wake of the destruction to wage war on local crime-lord Robert Latham. In the midst of this, Max Horton, The Wraith's right-hand man, vanishes without a trace. Searching for Max, and for those responsible for the devastation, The Wraith sets out for answers.

NOW AVAILABLE!

www.glowingeyesmedia.com

The Wraith Dread Avenger of the Underworld #4
CULT OF THE DAMNED
Frank Dirscherl

With the city back firmly in his grasp, crime lord and entrepreneur Robert Latham is celebrating by bankrolling Metro City's 200th anniversary gala year, which includes the unveiling of a never-before-seen ancient Aztec stone carving—the Cortes Stone—at the City Gallery, a carving that has thrilled the scientific and artistic communities, but infuriated the monstrous Aztekoth.

NOW AVAILABLE!

www.glowingeyesmedia.com

CRY OF THE WEREWOLF

The Wraith Dread Avenger of the Underworld #5
CRY OF THE WEREWOLF
Frank Dirscherl

Having gone through ordeal after ordeal, Paul Sanderson (aka The Wraith Dread Avenger of the Underworld ®) and his love Leena Patterson, decide to take a long overdue vacation. However, their idyll is soon shattered by an attack by a creature nobody thought could possibly exist—a werewolf. Soon, an evil so heinous makes himself known, and only The Wraith could possibly defeat it.

NOW AVAILABLE!

www.glowingeyesmedia.com

SWAMP WITCH OF SATAN'S FOREST

The Wraith Dread Avenger of the Underworld #6
SWAMP WITCH OF SATAN'S FOREST

Frank Dirscherl & Ray MacKay

On their way home from their mountain vacation which was anything but, Paul Sanderson (aka The Wraith) and his love Leena Patterson are waylaid by a mysterious cry for help, and are unwittingly drawn into the forest—and the web—of the alluring Swamp Witch.

NOW AVAILABLE!

www.glowingeyesmedia.com

The Wraith Dread Avenger of the Underworld #7
VENDETTA
Frank Dirscherl

After having been betrayed by crime lord, Robert Latham, and defeated by The Wraith, Crossfire has returned to cause mayhem and carnage at every turn. His ultimate aim? The utter destruction of all his enemies, and he doesn't care who gets in his way.

NOW AVAILABLE!

www.glowingeyesmedia.com

The Wraith Dread Avenger of the Underworld #9
KINGDOM
Frank Dirscherl

Crime lord, Robert Latham has returned, seemingly from the dead, ready to reclaim his kingdom. Ready to take whatever steps are necessary to restock and rebuild, to recover his rightful position within Metro City, and he doesn't care who gets in his way.

NOW AVAILABLE!

www.glowingeyesmedia.com

The Wraith Dread Avenger of the Underworld
#11

BIRDS OF THE LIVING DEAD

Frank Dirscherl

The dead are being re-animated, marching through Metro City, causing carnage throughout. Can The Wraith figure out what is going on, fight this undead menace, and find whomever is responsible? And what of the giant vultures plaguing the city? All this and more in this masterful tale of suspense and adventure.

NOW AVAILABLE!

www.glowingeyesmedia.com

The Wraith Dread Avenger of the Underworld
#12
THE ACOLYTE
Frank Dirscherl

Crossfire is back and this time he is mad with vengeance. So mad, he thinks he is the true avenger of Metro City, and sets out to prove his superiority over The Wraith, victim after bloody victim. And what does Robert Latham have to do with all this? Find out in this latest masterpiece from retro pulp master, Frank Dirscherl.

COMING SOON!

www.glowingeyesmedia.com

Books of Judgment Book One
SANDERSON OF METRO
Frank Dirscherl & Bobby Nash

Two masters of the pulp fiction world, Frank Dirscherl and Bobby Nash, have come together to tell this tale, the secret NEVER before told origin of the first Wraith/Paul Sanderson, as only they could. This action-packed, atmospheric thrill could only be told now, and it could only be told by master storytellers like Dirscherl and Nash. An epic never to be repeated and not to be missed.

NOW AVAILABLE!

www.glowingeyesmedia.com

Books of Judgment Book Two
SERPENT RISING
Frank Dirscherl & Greg Gick

The never-before-told origin story of The Wraith's arch nemesis the
Cobra. Who he is, how he came to be, and how his and the
original Paul Sanderson's life intertwined at key moments to cause
them to become deadly adversaries. It's all here!

NOW AVAILABLE!

www.glowingeyesmedia.com

RISING SON
BOOKS OF JUDGMENT

Books of Judgment Book Three
RISING SON
Frank Dirscherl & Adam Oravec

Robert Latham, Metro City's pre-eminent businessman and entrepreneur. He's also the head of the largest crime cartel on the east coast, the web in the center of the city's web of evil. But how did he become the all-powerful figure within the city. Growing up with nothing, he built his empire from the ground up, through strength, determination, and cold-blooded intimidation.

COMING SOON!

www.glowingeyesmedia.com

About the Type

Garamond is a group of many old-style serif typefaces, originally those designed by Parisian craftsman Claude Garamond and other 16th century French engravers, and now many modern revivals. Though his name was written as 'Garamont' in his lifetime, the typefaces are generally spelled 'Garamond'. **Garamond Normal**, used in this book, is one of those modern revivals.

Join FRANK DIRSCHERL and LEN DRISCOLL with Glowing Eyes Media on social media!

facebook.com/glowingeyesmedia

@glowingeyesmedia

instagram.com/glowingeyesmedia

@glowingeyesmedia.bsky.social

glowingeyesmedia.proboards.com

All Glowing Eyes Media, The Wraith, George 'Magpie' Collins novels, comics and merchandise can be obtained directly from the Glowing Eyes Media website –
www.glowingeyesmedia.com